Theft

# ff

# RACHEL INGALLS

## Theft

*faber and faber*
LONDON · BOSTON

First published in 1970 by
Faber and Faber Limited
3 Queen Square  London WC1N 3AU

First Faber Paperback edition
published in 1986
Printed and bound in Great Britain by
Redwood Burn Limited, Trowbridge, Wiltshire

© Rachel Ingalls 1970

ISBN 0 571 13991 4

"Look out, Jake," I said, "there's a big stone in the middle of the road."

"Where?"

"Straight ahead, right in front of you. Hold on. Over to the left a little ways. Mind you don't bump into it."

"Can't bump into it. Can't even see it."

"Right up there." I pointed at it in the dark. "A big goddam boulder, right in the middle of the road. Who'd want to put a thing like that there?"

"Where?"

"Right there, right in front of you," I said, and fell over it.

"Where are you?" he started to call. "Hey, where did you go?"

"I'm down here. By this big boulder."

"What boulder?" he muttered. And he fell on top of me.

"Jake, I think maybe I'm drunk," I said.

"Who, me? I'm not drunk."

"Me. Do you think I'm drunk?"

"I don't know. Do you think so?"

"I believe maybe I just might be. Just a little."

"Let's have another," he said. "Where did it go?"

"I think you're sitting on it."

We had another, and then another. And one more. And he said for about the tenth time that night, "Well, how's it feel to be a father?"

"Fine. Feels good. Feels grand. God almighty, I'm glad it's over."

"Nothing to it. I told you it was going to be all right, didn't I?"

"Sure. It's all right now. But wait till it happens to you. Man, I been scared before. Not like that."

"Why scared? Happens every day. That's nature. Annie says she'll be aiming for eight. Eight, she says. At least."

"Eight. Holy God."

"What she says. And I want to be there when it happens."

"You're crazy."

"Why not? That's life. That's important. I'd want to be there."

"Let me tell you," I said, and I thought I was going to start crying, but it came out laughing, "let me tell you, it was almost death. They said she almost died. I'm so glad it's over, I'm just so damn glad it's over."

"Have another," Jake said.

I took some and held on to it.

"Listen. You want to be there when it happens? Look, I wasn't even there and I felt like you can't imagine what. All week I been all cramped up and sick with it, like I was the one having the child. You just don't know. Here, have another."

I passed it to him and he dropped it and we had to hunt around.

"Got it," Jake said after a while. "What you doing going dropping it right on the ground like that? I thought you was handing it over."

"You dropped it."

"Who, me? It's all right. Plenty left."

"Have another."

"Don't mind if I do."

I leaned my back against the rock. It was still so dark you couldn't see much.

6

"Well?" Jake said.

"Well what?"

"You said have another. Let's have it."

"You're holding on to it."

"Who, me?" he said. After a little he began to laugh. I didn't know what was so funny but I started to laugh too.

"You're right," he said. "I had a hold of it all the time. Do you think maybe I'm drunk?"

"Who, me?" I said.

"Here, have another. How's it feel to be a father?"

We both got laughing. When we stopped it was at the same time, so it sounded very still afterwards. I felt quiet and better.

"I'll tell you, Jake," I said. "It's quite something. It makes you feel strange. I expect you get used to it, but it makes you feel like—makes you feel real awestruck. When you think about it, it's a big thing."

"Sure. Sure is. I'll drink to that. What are you going to name him?"

"I think we'll have to name him after Uncle Ben."

"You ain't going to name him after me?"

"I wanted to, but Maddie said how it would mean so much to him and Annie says she thinks it's right, seeing how he practically brought us up."

"I was only fooling."

"No, I meant it. I did want to. We'll name the next one after you."

"Right. And we'll name one after you, too."

"One of the eight."

"I'll drink to that," he said. We both drank some more and sat quiet for a while. I got to thinking how good it was to have the worry over but how funny we should be sitting in the middle of the dark, in the middle of the road, up against a big boulder that shouldn't be there.

7

"Hey Jake, I don't know about this rock. Who'd want to go and do a thing like that?"

"Like what?"

"Go and put a big rock in the middle of the road like that, where somebody can come along and get hurt. I think we should push it out of the way."

I gave it a shove but it was too heavy to move. I tried again and my hand slipped.

"Leave it be," he told me. "Wait till daylight and I'll help you move it."

"All right. All right, we'll leave it. Let's have another."

"Funny it should make such a difference—names. You remember when I used to tell you the names of the stars?"

"Sure," I said. "I remember."

"Funny it should make such a difference. Why people remember a name a long time after they'll remember anything else, after they forget what went with it. Did you ever think: names are very old things. Old as the stars. Pass them down from way back, and then people give them to children when they're born. Funny way to start out."

"I've forgotten most of them," I said.

"Which?"

"Names of the stars. A long while back. I was ashamed to say, because of all the trouble you took and then me going and forgetting."

"That's all right. Everybody does. Remember some things and forget some things. I'll teach you again sometime. Not tonight. No stars tonight. It's going to rain."

"We'll name the second one after you," I said.

"Right. And we'll name one after you. The first boy. Unless Annie's got some name she won't give up."

"You mean it?"

"Sure," he said. "Promise."

He fell asleep first. During the night it rained and when

8

daybreak came we saw that we weren't in the middle of the road; there wasn't any road at all. We were lying in somebody's field, miles from home and feeling like nothing on God's earth. I've only been drunk twice in my life and that was the first time. Almost eight years ago.

"You," the foreman calls, "you there, boy, you dreaming?"

"No, sir," I say.

I'm not dreaming, I'm just trying to stay on my feet. If I could dream it through I would, right on through the day. What I do is more like just thinking or remembering, anything to take my mind off being hungry. I didn't start on it till after the fire and now I have to do it every day.

It's best if you can do it to singing or to counting, out loud. The new man gets nervous if there's too much of the singing, he thinks every song he doesn't know might be a protest song. Up he walks in his Godalmighty way like he's saying to himself: here I come, boys, here I come. And tells us not so much of the singing, it slows down the work.

I can do it in my head now and I expect it's what happens to soldiers; they say soldiers can be sound asleep and still keep on marching once they've got the rhythm. That's the way it happens. Sometimes I begin by saying over words to myself. Or names, or following the line of a song without sounding it. Then I can imagine pictures of things, people, or places, and go on from there. Just remembering back a week will often take you into a string of things you haven't thought about for a long while, and they can keep you going.

I think about my mother's voice sometimes. She could sing. And I think about my father, though only a couple of memories and they're like the ones of her, blurred and hard to get at. I remember looking into his face but not what the face looked like. I remember being held in his arms and being small enough to be held like that. Clearest of all, I have a picture of being out walking with him. He lifted me up and

9

carried me on his shoulders—that's all I remember of it, like a picture I can stand away from and look at: me riding on his shoulders and looking up ahead, seeing the sky. But it's very strong and always when I think of him it leads me into other thoughts, I think how I did the same thing with Ben when he was smaller.

They say he was a great man, at least that's what everyone said till after Aunt Mary died. Then Uncle Ben started saying, "Yes, he was a great man all right, such a fine character, such high principles. He was such a great man and had such strong principles your Mama died of work." A long time later I said to him, "I don't know what he was like, I was too young. Aunt Mary saw him one way, you saw him another way—leave it like that. I only saw him like a child, I only remember him lifting me up on his shoulders and looking at the sky."

"Yes, that's what he was like," says Uncle Ben in a bitter voice. "He'd lift you up and show you the sky. Some it cured and some was killed by it."

I don't know if he was such a high-principled character. Maybe he was just wild, like Jake. And a man people would always be talking about, with a kind of public reputation. Like Jake; I've seen him walk down the street and have people come up and follow him, follow him around like dogs, just to be near him. And I've seen it the other way around, name-calling when he walks by, and the kids rushing out to throw a stone after him as soon as he's out of range.

After the fire Jake asked me, "You haven't been joining any of those freedom organizations, have you?"

"No, I thought that was your field. You still fighting for our racial equality?"

He didn't answer one way or the other, just said again, "You sure about that?"

It might have been. They asked me to, all right, kept

hanging around, trying to sound me out and talking: injustice, freedom, exploitation of labor, all those things. I didn't let on what my political views were, just told them the truth: that I didn't have the time to join anything no matter how good the cause. I know those boys—sit around talk, talk, talk and when they're through doubletalking each other, out they go and beat up some poor fool who's just trying to make an honest living and never did nobody harm. I don't spell freedom like that.

They went away and a couple of weeks later came back a second time. Then they tried to bribe me. Dragged in Maddie and the kids and said what a better life they'd lead and so on. So I told them: Look, I had all those milk and honey lies from the competition and I'm not buying, thanks all the same. And I told them to beat it.

I don't think it was that, but you can't tell about these things any more.

"Just asking," he says. "It don't seem like it could have been accidental."

And I said, "Look, Jake, strange as it may seem, working your guts out from the age of sixteen on don't leave a man much time for long discussions on what we're all going to do when we rule the world. What do you think, now?"

He said it looked to him like a pretty unprofessional job but he'd ask around. Maybe it was a freak thing, a mistake, or what Annie said: "Maybe just somebody wanting to put you out of action so they could get their hands on that famous job of yours." I can believe that. She laughed when I took her seriously, but I don't think it's at all unlikely. Anyway, it couldn't have come from very high up otherwise Jake would have found out, working with one foot on each side of the line like he does.

"What's that you're doing there, dreaming?" says the foreman.

"No, sir."

"We don't pay you to just stand around with your mouth open catching flies."

He's got a neck like a bull, a thick bulge at the back under his hair. Not muscle; that's fat. Fat from forty years of over-eating.

"Hustle it on up there," he says.

"Yessir."

The second time I got drunk was with a stranger, an old man they called Little Josh. It was the year of the big riot when they first started calling the army in and I first heard what martial law meant, that if you show yourself you're a dead man and they say you were looting. I'd lost my job and went to work with the fruitpickers. I walked all night to get there so I wouldn't lose a day's work and worked on through as soon as I arrived. I've never seen people work like that, sometimes through half the night, because we were paid by the basketload, and falling asleep under the trees whenever it hit them. There were some women there and children too. A lot of knifings in the night, a lot of drinking, and one night a man hung himself from a tree and nobody noticed, they worked all around him till daylight. That was the first time I'd seen a hanged man: mouth open, tongue out, swollen, suffocated.

We were allowed to eat all the fruit we wanted and I couldn't believe it to begin with because we can't afford to buy it at home. It tasted so sweet, the way you imagine flowers would taste, but if you try to live off it you get sick. Some of the women there set up stands where they sold bread and fish fried in oil, and now whenever there's fish being fried it reminds me of that time, being bone-tired, sleeping on the ground, and the smell of the fruit and trees everywhere, even in your clothes.

The second week I was there an old man joined the group;

he was short and had a squashed-in face and walked leaned-over a little, which made his arms look longer than they should be. He stood looking at the trees, ready to choose his workplace, and somebody made a remark. A few others joined in and soon there was about seven of them poking fun at him. "That's all right, Grandaddy," I said to him. "Don't pay them no mind. You work along with me." I pointed out my place, we walked over to it, and started in. Little Josh he was called, and I couldn't believe he only had two hands—he was picking nearly twice as much as anybody else.

The night we got drunk everyone was eating and drinking in an abandoned place up on a rise in the land. There were still some walls standing, a few stone steps up the hill, and a lot of roots growing through it all. I remember they had fires going, cooking, and I was being eaten alive by the bugs. When we left five men came and leaned over the edge of the wall to see if I'd fall down the steps. I turned around and said, "You think I'm going to fall down, don't you?" One of them said yes, the others said they just wanted to see we were all right. "Well, I'm not going to," I said, turned back around, and nearly fell down the steps. Little Josh had the same amount and he was still sober long after everybody else was blind. There was a full moon out. And stars. He told me next day that before I passed out I'd pointed out the stars to him, naming them in a very loud voice as if they were being given names for the first time.

I only started thinking this last week about being drunk. Because it's the same feeling; not the happy lifted-up feeling while you're drinking. Like what you feel when you wake up afterwards: shaky, tired, and your head hurts. That's what going hungry is like.

That morning I left before Maddie could ask me what I'd eat. I had the feeling if I didn't get up on my feet quick and start walking, I'd fall down. I got to work early, which they never notice, only if you come late. And it was so bad I couldn't even work the trick with thinking and remembering.

It was a Thursday. They got us both on the same day, two hours apart between the two arrests.

Naturally, if I'd known about Jake I'd never have tried it on my own. But there were all those weeks behind me, of Maddie asking "what did you eat at midday", and me telling her lies. The first few days it was easy to make up a pretend meal. Later I'd begin to repeat.

"You had that yesterday," she says.

"So?"

"Are you sure you're eating all right? You can't stint yourself with the work you're doing. You'll get sick. Then where will we be?"

"You quit fussing. I'm eating fine," I say, and it was a lie again. I hardly ever ate lunch since the fire, when we lost the livestock.

Then I'd ask her what she and the kids had had. She'd say they'd had the leftovers from the night before. One evening that week I say, "Isn't this what we had last night?"

"Yes. You don't like it?"

"I thought you said you finished it off at lunch."

"There was a lot left over," she said.

Sure. Believe it every time. The children aren't getting any fatter, either, and that means she goes without hers altogether. I saw them from the field one day, off in the distance a lot of kids scrabbling around the ditches over by the spring. But I recognized my two. And the foreman, seeing me look, said, "What some folks will allow, letting it get so the children got to go digging in the ditches, eating the weeds

14

out of the creek. Their folks should be ashamed. Letting them run loose on private property like that."

"Yessir," I said, and knew for certain then that Maddie was lying too.

"That's theft. That's what those children will grow up to," he says. "It's the parents' fault. That's what's wrong with all the young people nowadays—their parents don't set them an example. I'd give those kids a good hiding, you can bet, if I was their father."

"Yessir," I said. And I can believe it. Because nobody ever burned you out and taxed you into the ground. I can see you beating your own kids for being hungry. Bet you're real thick with the tax men. Never had to say "Yes, sir" while you were hungry right down to your bones and saw your children starve.

I used to walk through the market at midday. It's amazing how the bare smell of food can keep you going. Even watching somebody else eat sometimes helps, though you wouldn't think it. And even more curious is the way a real meal in the evening, if you take it slow, can be invested with the taste of the best things you could wish for.

Sometimes at the end of the day I'd beg scraps off the tradespeople in the square. They were good about it, they knew how it was. But at noon you couldn't ask since they had to make their living too, and sell as much as they could before the end of the day. The soldiers had plenty of food of course, and kids used to hang around them, pick up whatever they threw away. That might have been a good idea for me to try. Yet I never did know a soldier who'd dish out so much as a crust to a grown man, though he'd give anything to a child. Part of it may be natural sentiment, but I believe they also consider it actually unlucky to refuse a child. Say no to a man and the only had luck is his own that you refused.

That afternoon in the market I couldn't stand it any longer. The weeks seemed like months, and while I thought that, began to seem like years. All the way through in my chest and legs and belly I could feel all of that time I'd gone without food.

It was bread set out to cool. And I smelled it from a long way off. From beyond the fruit and vegetable stands and the basketware it led me, pulled me, right through the crowd. Sweet and warm, giving off fragrance like a tree in bloom.

If Jake had been along he'd have known how to handle the situation. He says just never give your right name and you'll be all right. With the political atmosphere like it is they'll never bother to pick you up on the street again unless they recognize you. And that's unlikely, because they think we all look alike. Or if it's one of ours working for them, chances are he'll let it go unless it's for something so big that he'd get a recommendation out of it.

Jake was very relaxed when he toted things off. He knew all the right lies to tell, and the right names to say, and he'd state with great confidence that so-and-so had sent him to collect the article because he had an account there. "Oh, aren't you Mr. so-and-so and isn't this such-and-such a street?" he'd ask. And then he had a charming manner of apologizing while he handed the thing back, and a self-assured way of asking directions as to how to get to the mythical place he'd mentioned.

I'd never done it before myself.

I walked blind, straight to it. I saw it sitting there, fresh and new as a baby, and just put my hand on it like it belonged to me, and walked off with it.

I hadn't taken but ten steps before there was a hand on my shoulder and the law and the military were standing all around.

"Where'd you get that?" one of them said.

I started to eat the bread because I was goddamned if I was going to go to prison and be punished and all the rest for something I hadn't even enjoyed.

"What are you doing there?" said a second one.

I kept cramming the bread into my mouth, all new and sweet and soft, and thought: whatever comes now, whatever else happens, it's been worth it.

"Cut that out, you. That's stolen property you've got there," said the first one.

I kept on eating.

"Leave go, I said," the first one told me.

They began to push. I got my face into the bread and had my elbows working, but in the end it was more of a fight than I could manage without my fists and anyway they kicked the remainder out of my hands. About half the bread was left; during the scuffling they stepped all over it till it flattened out into the ground.

They punched me in the head just as routine procedure and kicked me a couple of times the way I've seen them do to other people, and took me off. Theft, resisting arrest, and striking an officer in the pursuit of his duty. They told me the charge on the way. The younger one seemed very impressed by the sound of it. He kept jerking my arm up behind me while they dragged me along, and saying, "Oh, you're in trouble. Are you in trouble. Are you ever."

They took me all the way into the center of town. First they made me wait while they talked over what they were going to do with me. I think that lasted about an hour but I'm not sure, because it was like I gave up time as soon as I knew it was all really happening and jail at the end of it. Then one of them said, "All right, that's it," and they took me outside again and to the prison.

It was one of the old-fashioned kind, going all the way down into the ground below floor-level. Some of the building consisted of the original solid rock. And they put me down, under ground, into a room where the cells were hewn right out of the stone. No windows, only a view through bars into the center of the place where the jailer and a friend sat at a table and threw dice.

The first person I noticed when they brought me in was Jake. He didn't say anything, so I gave no sign and was glad I'd told them a false name.

There were six cells in all. Two big high-ceilinged ones on either side of the entrance, then two on each of the side walls. It was really a triangle-shaped place; the side walls came together in a point of rock and the roof sloped down at the join. The ceiling was also stone and gave you the feeling that at one time the whole thing had been a big natural cave with hollows. Jake was in one of the small end cells and they stuck me in the other one, so we were next to each other but almost close enough to touch, and because of being at the triangle-point where the side walls met, we could see each other's faces.

It wasn't too bad. High enough so the top just cleared my head when I stood up straight, though it was smaller and lower near the far wall, with hardly room for your head if you were sitting down.

The jailer went back to the entrance where he stood around talking to the soldiers. His friend followed after, lingered for a time, and then went out. I had a feeling he was supposed to be on duty someplace else and was making a retreat while the jailer kept the others busy. They were all in uniform, the jailer and his friend, too.

"Did you give your right name?" Jake said.

"No."

"That's the style."

"What did they get you for?"

"Stole a horse."

"A whole horse? What for?"

"Not to eat, you fool. To plow. One of the horses they were using for crowd control. I had a buyer lined up and everything. Had it walking behind me quiet as you please when that fake beggar on the corner—you know, by the fruit-juice stand—"

"I know him. Paid informer."

"Oh, I know that. I been paying him too. But it looks like yesterday the military priced him out of my range, because he was the one pointed me out."

It sounded like small-time stuff, not the kind of thing Jake would let happen. But I know he still picks things up now and then just to keep his hand in, he says, and for fun.

"Bad luck," I said.

"He'll think so if I get out."

"What do you mean if?"

He tapped his foot against the wall.

"This place feels damn solid. Looks like some kind of security prison. Four armed men standing behind the jailer when he opens up to give you your provisions. Not so easy. Not so easy at all. I never been in one like this before."

"But they'll have to take us out to be tried."

"Tie us hand and foot, like as not."

"Do they usually do that? I thought you said these boys were pretty easy-going."

"Not any more." He kicked the wall again.

"Hell, all I did was steal a little bit of bread."

"Bread? Caught out for lifting a hunk of bread? Oh, Seth, goddamn. You fool, you."

"All right, all right. They got you too, didn't they?"

"Why didn't you wait till I was with you? A beginner's trick like that. I don't suppose you even thought of going up to it with your coat over your arm."

"No, I never thought of that," I said. "I'll remember."

"You do that. And you can remember never try it alone, too. Not till you got somebody to show you how. Lord, whatever possessed you?"

"I was just hungry as hell."

"Why didn't you ask me for a loan?"

"Cut it out."

"Why not? We've got plenty."

I didn't want to go into all that again. We've borrowed enough off him already. Sure, he's got plenty till they catch him for getting it. And the more he gives away, the more he's got to go against the law.

I said, "Listen, Jake, what with the last time I paid any taxes and what you gave us after the fire, that's more than any man should be asked to lend."

"I'm not any man. I'm kin. You should have asked me."

Sure. The way things stood I wouldn't be able to pay back what he'd already given us. Not for years. Maybe never.

"Let's stop talking about it. It makes me sick to think about it."

"And what about Maddie? And the kids? Maddie says—"

"What?"

His face changed and he shut his mouth. So she'd asked him. She never told me.

"Well," I said, "how much is it now?"

"She didn't want you to know. Don't tell her I said anything. I'm glad to give it, Seth. Honest. I worry about you."

"I'm all right."

"No you are not."

"You're right, I'm not."

"A long time ago somebody told you honesty's the best policy. And you been sticking to it a long time after you figured out honesty's the fastest way to starvation."

"And dishonesty lands you in jail."

20

"Only if you get caught."

"Well?" I said. "Well?"

I grabbed hold of the bars and gave them a shake. Built for keeps. They were solid as a mountain wall.

One of the soldiers out beyond the entrance laughed. I could just see them around the corner. They were drinking together and the jailer appeared to be telling them a tall tale of some sort, acting out the different voices as the story went on. One of the men wiped his mouth with the back of his hand and said something that made the rest of them laugh too. They weren't looking in our direction.

"Do they beat you up or anything?"

"Not yet. I don't think it's likely. The jailer's all right. He's a good man."

"He looks like some kind of a clown."

"He is," Jake said, "but he's all right."

I began to wonder what would happen to Maddie; whether she'd have enough to live on, whether she'd guess what had happened to me, or think I'd been killed, or maybe think I'd left her. She couldn't be thinking that.

"Listen, Jake. If I try to get word to Maddie, they'll find out my name, won't they?"

"That's all right. You just leave it. Sam, you know Sam, he saw me when the law came on the scene. He'll tell Annie. She'll come over here and she'll see you, then she'll tell Maddie."

"You think she'll be all right?"

"Sure, Annie will see she's all right. She'll look after them."

"I just wish I could see her, right now. They'll let her come see me?"

"Sure. It'll take a while for the word to go around."

I thought of her sitting at home in the evening, waiting for me to come back from work. I imagined the kids asking questions when it began to get later and later and still I didn't come. And what her face would look like when Annie told her, what she'd say: not this on top of everything else. And when she finally came to visit me, looking through the bars, any other woman would say: How could you, how could you be so foolish or so selfish or so cruel to us, as if we didn't have enough trouble already. But she would ask me if I was all right, if I was well.

"I don't know if I can face her," I said.

"Well, what do you want? First you're scared she won't be able to come, then you don't think you can face it."

He told me I never should have taken up crime in my old age, you had to start young while you still had a sense of humor. He was smiling, the way I'd seen him look at Annie when she sulked, but harder.

"I bet the job's gone," I said. "Bet somebody else is doing my work right now."

"Most likely."

"I never missed a day in nine years. Not even when I was sick."

"That was your trouble."

Outside the entrance it sounded as though the group of men was beginning to break up. Two of them went down the hall and the jailer leaned around the corner and gave Jake a friendly kind of look. Jake nodded to him and started to talk again, but he dropped his voice.

"Tell you the truth, Seth, most of these jailhouse shacks you can bust through the wall with your thumbnail, but this one is over my head. I tell you, I never seen one like this before, not even the military cells. And I don't like it. I think something's going on. You been listening to the news lately?"

"Politics, you mean?"

"We got them on the run, looks like. Arrests going on in batches, in bundles. All this week they've been clamping

22

down. All along the line. And it's started up at the top somewheres. Scared stiff. I don't believe there's one empty jail in town."

"You think they put us in here just because they don't have room anyplace else?"

"Could be. I hope that's why. Hope it ain't because they think we're special. You haven't been joining any of those freedom organizations, have you?"

"You asked me that once before already."

"I wonder maybe did somebody burn you out because you joined something or other. I wondered at the time."

"Because I didn't join, maybe. They asked me."

"Oh, my Lord. And you refused. So that's it. What did you tell them?"

"Just told them to go to hell."

"I see. Did you ever hear from them again?"

"Nope. They had somebody follow me a while back, about five months ago, but he never spoke to me and at least nobody was hanging around the kids or Maddie, which really would've had me scared. He just used to dog me around the place, him and a friend. They didn't even stick very close except in crowds, so they wouldn't lose me. And then they quit all of a sudden, about five months back, like I say."

"Sounds all right. Makes sense."

"You don't think there's a connection, do you? That they were just waiting to arrest me?"

"No, not any more. Not if that's all there was to it. I was just thinking about the time element. No, you're in the clear there. They've got better things on their minds by now, I expect."

Worse things, I'd say. I've seen some of those men around town. In the crowds. All last week and the week before, when there's that feeling in the crowd, sort of agitated but just

23

waiting, like kindling about to go up, I've spotted them.

He said, "Something's happening for sure. I mean something more than what I know already. A lot of people are keeping their mouths shut that never used to."

From the entrance I heard steps and the sound of something being moved, maybe a table. The jailer came in and walked over to us. He was a stumpy gingery man, going bald at the front; large in the shoulder and walked with a bit of a limp and a funny rolling, like he might have been a navy man. He rubbed his hands together and gave me a big smile through the bars.

"Hungry?" he shouted. "Food!"

I couldn't believe it. I thought it might be the beginning of one of those mental tortures you hear about.

"You no want? No hungry today?"

"Yes, sure. I'm hungry."

"Good-good-fine."

He said it all in one breath and he had a funny way of talking, like he was putting on an accent or something. He smiled again and thumped his chest.

"Homer, that's me. Foreigner. My mother she is Greek, but I been citizen a long time now—fully qualified reliable citizen, keep the law. But I know, you know—before. Before I'm so respectable, I been on the other side of the bars, your friend Adam can tell you."

"Adam?"

"Oh, so sorry, I think you friends already." He jerked his thumb at Jake. "Adam," he said, and then nodded his head at me and said, "Abe."

"How do," Jake muttered, and glared at me.

24

"I hear you talking and I think you know each other already."

"Just passing the time of day," Jake said.

"Yes, is good. So I put you next door. Is sad, it make you worry behind bars when you get nobody to talk to. Is true, yes? Me, I talk all the time."

"It's the poet in him," Jake said. "Tells me he's got poetic ancestors, ain't that right?"

"My name," said the jailer. "Is name of greatest poet of Greece. Homer. You know Homer?"

"Can't say as I do," I said, "but I never been out of the country. This Homer a big man over there in Greece?"

"Biggest. Biggest poet we got. But he is dead a long time. He lived hundreds of years before now, centuries before now. We got other poets, but Homer he is the best. You got poets too?"

"I expect. Fraid I don't know much about it."

"Sure," Jake said. "Everybody's got poets. But it's always the same story—the good ones died a long time ago and the ones we got now aren't any good. Five hundred years from now people will say somebody was the poet of his time today and it'll be some poor fool you never heard of. Must be a hard life living five hundred years faster than everybody else. I'd just as soon leave it alone."

"Ah but the glory!" says Homer.

"Sure. You figure it out. These poets and people don't begin to live till they're dead. So think about it: who's got all this glory? Dead men. Right? You can keep that. Besides, all the best poets are anonymous anyhow."

"Anonymous," says Homer, like he was trying out the sound of it.

"Seems to me if you're going to be a great man, be one in the world, where it counts. If you're looking for glory. Life after death ain't the kind of glory I'd be interested in."

25

"Your friend Adam, he is a philosopher, isn't it?"

"No," I said, "he's just got a good line and likes a fight."

"Is what I mean. Same thing. Got a good line, like a fight, it's what I call philosophy."

He turned and walked back to the entrance and yelled at someone outside. A voice answered back and he called again. This time it was probably an order, since nobody said anything but there was a lot of moving around.

"Adam?" I said. "What the hell?"

"Damn, you fool. See to it you don't mess up on it again."

"What kind of a joker is that anyway?"

"I told you, he's all right."

"I just hope he wasn't joking about the food."

"No, that's for real. They fed me once already."

"When did they pick you up?"

"An hour before noon, about then. They brought me straight here, even gave me a drink. It's all right. When did they get you?"

"About two hours after. But they dragged me around first, took me to about three different places inside this big building and made me wait."

"Did they ask you a lot of questions—I mean specific questions about people you know or business you might be involved in?"

"Just name, age, and where I lived. Most of the time I think they were arguing about who was responsible for me and whether I should be charged according to where I said I lived or where they made the arrest or what. Then I believe there was some complication about the charge being under the civil administration or the military authority—is that right? I wasn't paying much attention, I was all beat out. Does that have something to do with the trial, whether we'll be tried under some kind of martial law? I always thought martial law just meant they killed on sight."

"Did you find out which one they charged you under?"
Jake said.

"I don't rightly know."

What I remembered most about the waiting was the young
soldier who'd been set to keep an eye on me. He was the one
who hadn't dared to beat me up too openly, but while we
waited he went stiff as a plank with the strain, hoping I'd
make a move so he could watch the others come kick my
guts out. I kept wondering what sort of a man he'd be in
five years' time, whether he had a girl or a mother, whether
he wouldn't want her to see what his face looked like looking at me. Or if there was some person, anybody, for him
who he wouldn't ever want to find out exactly how he was
wishing the hurt on me, not out of hate but just to see it
happen.

I smelled food.

It came around the entranceway and filled the place like a
rain-bearing wind. The jailer came in, with four others and
the food. Jake told me quickly not to try for a break.

"The one on the left is mean as hell. I think I've seen him
around before, he's probably a retired professional fighter.
And Homer's a lot stronger than he looks—got me in the
neck when I made a move last time. Don't try it."

They opened the door, made me stand back so I had to
crouch down against the wall, and they set it all down on the
floor. Then they closed up again.

The smell was so good and so strong it made me dizzy. I
sat down with my back to the bars and took the bowl on my
knees, telling myself all the time to take it slow or it would
make me sick. I don't think I'd seen so much food together
in one meal for two years. It almost made me feel like crying.
And when I took the first mouthful it felt all surprised, as
though I'd just eaten it ten times over in my thoughts and
the taste of it should be different. They'd given us something

to drink, too, like Jake said they would. With every swallow I kept reminding myself to go slow, and hoping I wouldn't get so drunk I'd forget to call him Adam or that I was supposed to be Abe.

"How you doing, Abe?"

I turned my face around to him.

"Fine."

"If you could see what you look like. My, like you just been through some kind of mystical experience."

"If I'd known—if I'd known I was going to eat like this, I'd have *tried* to get in."

"It's just good luck," he said. "We're lucky to have Homer. All the jails I been in, nobody ever gave me food like this. See, the jailers get this allowance from the state for feeding prisoners. Most of them just pocket it. And some of them work it double, take the money and claim they get in more prisoners in a week than they've seen in a month. As busy making up names as we are. The officers are in on it too most times, or they know about it and let it go till they need a favor. I told you, Homer is all right. He don't even hold it against me for trying to break."

It took a long time and I was full before the bowl was empty, but I hung on to it and kept chewing real slow and washing it down between mouthfuls. Then I wondered about what to do afterwards. The only thing in the cell besides me and the walls was a straw mat at the back. And there was a funny, close smell about the place that I hadn't noticed so much while I'd been standing.

"Jake," I said, "you know, it isn't all that strong, but this place smells like they been keeping wild animals in it."

"That's us, society's wild animals."

"What do I—"

"Adam, Adam," he added. "Lord, will you remember it? You may be in the clear politically, but I'm not so sure they'd like it if they knew a few things I'd been up to lately. It's all right this time, he didn't hear. Just remember."

For a moment I thought the food would come up. I began to sweat and as soon as I felt it coming out I knew I'd been sweating in waves ever since they closed the cell door the first time.

"Sure," I said. "I'm sorry. I'm just not used to—"

"Take it easy. Don't get all panicked. What were you saying?"

"Oh, about what you do when you've got to relieve yourself in this place, just do it against the wall or where?"

"Ask Homer, he'll hand you a pot for it. I figure it's his own idea—I've got a mark on the wall over here and drawings by about five ex-prisoners. They never had it so good in this place till they hired Homer."

The whole bunch came back and we went through the unlocking again so they could take away the bowl and all, and I asked Homer.

"When he gives it to you," Jake says, "take it in the hand you aren't going to use to eat with, and then don't put that hand near your mouth again till you can wash it. Wipe it on your clothes if you have to. Be on the safe side."

"What do you mean?"

"What I say. And another thing, I haven't exactly seen anything moving yet, but I'd stay away from that straw job if you can help it. If you want to sleep, curl up on the floor near the bars."

"Not exactly the comforts of home."

"It's pretty good compared to the others. In that respect, at least."

He didn't say anything about the walls or even look at them, but he was thinking about them. I didn't mind for the moment. It went in patches, thinking about what was going to happen to us, and sweating, and then putting it

29

out of my mind. Right then I was thinking about Maddie again.

Later on Homer came in. He gave me the pot and some water and came back again a spell later and stayed to talk. He told us all kinds of stories from all over the world and had us both laughing. It was going fine between us and I was feeling good, almost proud about saying Adam or just leaving out the name every time I wanted to say something to Jake. Once when Homer stepped away to speak to a man at the entrance Jake said his stomach turned over every time he thought I was about to come out with his name, but I was pretty sure I could handle it now. There was just one time where I suddenly felt bad, when Homer was in the middle of a story and I wondered if they were all his or whether he'd collected some of them from the men he'd been in charge of and if maybe some of those men had been put to death.

Jake started in then, and he was in good form. Nobody can tell a tall tale like Jake, specially the ones where you have to keep a straight face till the end, and he had Homer wheezing and coughing and practically dancing over the floor with laughing.

I once said to Maddie I wished I was made like that, always joking and laughing and not taking the world seriously. And she said it only looked that way with Jake because he was so energetic and he'd always had that joking way and the gift to make other people laugh when he wanted them to. But really it was all put on like an actor, and underneath Jake was very serious. "A lot more than you," she said. But I never could see it, unless she meant political things. "Aren't I serious?" I said, and she'd said, "No, you're just worried," which was true enough.

I asked Homer finally, "Are you a navy man?"

"Who, me? No, not for anything would I go near the navy. Never."

"I just thought, no offense, the way you walk."

"Oh," he said, "oh, I break my ankle, is nothing. No, I get the choice a long time ago. You see, me and some others, they catch us for taking things. Oh, we were very young but we do it for years, all together working like a team. And the law says well you can choose how to be now, in a hole for life or you go into the forces. So what do I do? My mother is in the country illegal and I know so many boys die in the navy living so close like they do, freeze in the winter and burn up in the summer, wet all the time and no sleep—nothing. Three man I know kill themselves there. No, I don't touch the navy, is slavery. I say, I go into the army and serve the country, become a respectable citizen, earn money, travel maybe. And is what I do. Is not bad life, the army. And people have respect. Is no matter where you come from, how poor, if you're a good soldier you can put that behind. And other people also forget. Is democratic."

"Sure," said Jake. "Don't you think that's a damning indictment of a country, that the only way a man can become a first-class citizen or anything approaching it is to join the military? Though of course your case ain't quite the same as ours."

"You can join," Homer said. "Why not?"

"Why not? Oh, I know the army. But do they call it by its right name? Exploit a place here, free a place there—everybody's still at peace but meanwhile everyplace is being occupied and there are a lot of corpses lying around wherever the army's been. And if you look at the ordinary soldier, why, under normal conditions he'd be in the place of these people he's supposed to be guarding or freeing or occupying or whatever they call it from day to day. People with no rights.

He comes from someplace where he's got no rights and the army knows he'll join it to get hold of them. Then they make him take away the rights of other people just like him. I don't see how anybody can be such a—"

Suddenly he began to cover up. It sounded all right if you didn't know him and hadn't been looking for the pause before he started to unsay everything. I didn't think Homer would care in any case.

"Politics," Jake said. "I expect you've got politics in Greece, too."

"Don't speak of politics, she drive me crazy. All Greeks talk about politics, always. Always. Since beginning of time. We invent politics, I tell you."

He asked me if I held such strong views as my friend Adam.

"Not exactly," I said. "I sort of agree, but not for the same reasons. I got no grudge against the military, or the law either. Not really, when you think about it. I mean, somebody's got to keep order. But I don't know. I almost did join up with the forces, it sounded pretty good. Food and pay and travel maybe, all that. But I've seen too many folks go that way. They say it's such a wonderful life; follow the rules and work hard, and on your free time there's no responsibility and you're your own man. You get drunk and get into fights, have all the women you want, and nobody holds it against you. It's expected you're going to cut loose and go wild when the discipline lets up. Wherever you go there are always girls around and drink and everybody thinks you're so big because the army's big. Well, that's all right when you're eighteen or twenty or for a couple of years more. Gets the wildness out of you. But I've seen men, forty or fifty years old, and they're still leading that life and doing all those things, the things you do when you're eighteen or twenty, and still thinking that way: how good it is to be independent and tough and not be tied down. Those men, it's as if they never grew some-

32

how. And they're the ones that feel very strong about the army, get tears in their eyes when they remember how good it's been to them. Just because they've made the army into what they should have had if they were grown men. Work, get married, have a family and work for them—that's what a man should do."

"Lots of men in the army has families," Homer said.

"Sure, I know. The army'd rather have them single, though. And I was talking about career soldiers, that's what I'd have to be. Otherwise you get in there and get married, say, and then you can't get out because you need the pay twice as much, and what else are you fit for except soldiering if you've been in there for four or five years? You'd have to start right at the beginning and you can't do that because you got a family to support. And you're only half a family man besides, because you see more of the men you work with than you do of them. And when you get your time off, most of these men will try and talk you into going with them to hit the town, and they'll keep picking at you if you say no, tell you you're going soft, and make you think you're not a real man any more if you just want to have a quiet evening alone with your family. They're wrong. They're the ones don't know what it is to be a man. But it's hard to stand up to that kind of thing, especially if they're your friends, challenging your manhood like that. In the end you're only half a soldier and half married and you can't give your best to either side."

"You don't have to give the best," says Homer. "You act sensible and do not worry about the pride, it works out all right. Lots of soldiers have their families to live with them."

"And a lot of them only think it's going to work out easy that way and then find out it's harder than they imagine. The way things are, it's easy for army families to break up."

"But lots of men has their family come along and no trouble," says Homer.

"Sure, I know. The family ain't too happy about it, though. It takes a real solid marriage for it to work. Even then, I know of cases where they split up. It's just that you can only have the one or the other all the way. Sometimes it works out. That's mostly when the boys go in there for the money and save it up, send it home, and don't get married till they're out. But that's dangerous, of course. I could have done that, I suppose. Go in to fight, right into the front-liners—that's where the money is. But we were too poor to take the chance. Even allowing for me being scared to die, I couldn't afford to—no honest, it ain't so funny. Say I lasted two years and get killed, well what happens to my family in five or ten years? That means they're one worker short for the rest of their lives. And now I got a family of my own. I could have joined the military yesterday. Sometimes I got so desperate I thought I'd maybe do that. But the way the political situation is now, you know they'd never send me out of the country. I'd have more value to them here. They'd stick me right here in the middle of the city, keep me on home ground, so the next time there's a big riot I'd be out there doing crowd control. And who'd be in the crowd? Some day I might come face to face with my best friend or my wife or even my kids. So you see I can't, the choice isn't really there. It doesn't make sense to say I could join. I couldn't, not the way it's set up."

"You married?"

"Yes, married young. Are you?"

"Oh yes," Homer said. "But I'm not so young when I marry. She's back home. Across the water. I save to bring her over."

"A Greek girl?" Jake said.

"Girl?" Homer laughed. "I tell her, she like that." He drew a picture in the air with his hands, showing us his wife's shape. "A woman!" he said loudly. "A big woman, built big."

34

"Big as that?" said Jake. "That's something you can hang on to in a storm, all right."

"You bet," said Homer, and winked. We all laughed.

"Plenty storms in marriage, I guess. She is not beautiful. But I miss. She has a pretty voice, soft. And she is funny—no, is fun. Fun to talk with, not stupid. She make you feel good. Is most important of all, isn't it?"

"Yes," I said.

Jake shrugged and said he'd never thought about what was the most important thing of all.

"I got the one I wanted, anyway, that's important. Only I like them a little smaller."

He put his hands through the bars and shaped a curve out and in and out, and looked at me.

"What do you say, Abe?" he said.

I wondered what would he do if I came out with it and told him: I say that's my sister you're talking about so freely. He was enjoying himself, putting me on the spot when he knew there was a doubt about how far he could push me, and whether I'd remember his name right. It's strange to have a friend like that, so close you know each other like your one hand knows the other, but you don't understand, like I still don't understand how Jake doesn't worry or how it is he's got to walk right on the edge, always, and thinks it's fun.

He said, "I always found those big girls give you a lot of working space, but in the long run most of them are kind of low on activity. Make you do the whole job yourself. I like something with more action."

Homer leaned his hand up against the wall just far enough away so Jake couldn't grab him if he wanted, and said, "Is lots of men play the trumpet, but not all of them can make her sing."

"There's one on you, Adam."

35

Jake was smiling, and said, "That's pretty good. I'll have to remember that one."

"You married too?" Homer asked him.

"That's right."

"Children?"

"No."

"You?" he asked me.

"Two. A boy and a girl. One of each."

"Is good. Me too. My boy Alexander, twelve year old, and the little girl is ten, Cora. We disagree about the name, so we just call her Cora which means girl. My wife has a beautiful name, is Phyllis, which means a green bough."

"The which?"

"A green bough. How you name your children?"

"Ben, he's seven, going on eight. And Mary. She's, oh almost six now. Every time somebody asks me I have to think. They grow so fast. And my wife's name is Maddie, Madeleine."

"Madeleine, is nice. But you are young to have a boy eight year old."

"Twenty-five," I said. "I told you, I married young."

"You ever regret?"

"Not about that, no."

"Is very young," he said.

That's what they said when we got married. And afterwards somebody always says don't you have second thoughts about it now. I don't see it, like asking a man does he regret being a man, does he have second thoughts about his own family. Everything else could go, and does, and that's the bitterness. But if that went, that's your life, the people you love. Jake says it's freedom and ideas that move the world, but the men who keep pushing freedom and ideas know that's a lie, and if instead of just burning us out they'd tried to do something to Maddie and the kids, they could have had me doing what they said, for a while anyway, till I figured out how to stop it. They know that. They just must have thought I wasn't worth their time.

"It's been hard sometimes. It would have been harder alone."

"Twenty-five," said Homer. "If I was twenty-five again, oh, that is young. Me, I am forty-seven. Forty-seven."

"Old enough to be my old man."

"No," he said. "I was not here then."

He turned to Jake, who was laughing at what he'd said.

"You are older a little?"

I thought how funny it was that out of the two of us Homer liked Jake better, but I was the one that trusted Homer. I forget just when it was I began to trust him, but now I'd have told him anything about me and I didn't believe he'd carry it to anybody else. But Jake didn't trust him. He never trusted anybody unless he'd known them nearly all his life and even then you could count the ones he really trusted on your fingers. And there were things he wouldn't let people know just because he said it wouldn't be good for them to know.

"Oh, I'm bowed down with age compared to him."

"How old?" asked Homer, and Jake decided to tell him.

"Twenty-nine."

"Old? That is young. Very."

"Young for some, old for others. I'm no spring chicken any more."

"What's that?"

"Just a phrase. Means not in the first flush of youth, not green, not younger than most. Old Abe there is what you call green."

"Green?"

"Lacking in experience."

Homer thought about that and I thought: that's why he

likes Jake better, because of being experienced, which is true, though Maddie always said not to mind. That day after I lost my temper she said not to mind, she'd rather have a fool with a good heart any day than a worldly man who said bitter things. "He's what you call cynical," she said. "And you don't know what he's thinking. I know, when you get mad you just roar and break things and lash out, and when you think something you say it. But what it is he thinks, Jake never shows, not anything. It makes me nervous. I wonder it don't make Annie nervous. Maybe he shows it to her. I'd rather know where I stand." And I told her, "Annie knows where she stands, all right." That was early, when we were first married, and I was ashamed to lose my temper, I didn't believe it could happen where you were contented. Some little thing it was, and all my life I been careful not to get mad like that, because being stronger than most through the chest and arms and shoulders, you have to be careful or your own strength can turn against you and break you. Like I never like to get into fights or even be in crowds that might be about to demonstrate or something, I always try to avoid it, because I get that feeling once I was in I'd kill somebody. Or hurt somebody by mistake. And you can get so you like it, I've seen that happen too. Once when we were kids, I remember, hitting Jake harder than I'd thought, turning around and seeing the blood on his face, and it made me want to die. He didn't say a thing. It's as though you can't hurt him. And he still loves a fight, but not for anger. For fun. I know when he's angry: he gets very calm, his voice goes gentle, and it's worse than if he hit you or shouted or smashed something. Like that day he came in the door and he'd heard the rumor the neighbors started, saying the Lord had put a judgment on him for his way of life and that was why he and Annie didn't have any children and wouldn't ever. He put down something he was carrying and said very

38

quiet, it only took one spiteful tongue to take away the good name of a thousand people and what did it matter to him, what the hell. Annie tried to run out of the room but he caught her by the elbow going around the doorway and just said, "Let's have my dinner, it's been a long day."

We talked a little more and Homer left us for a while. He said there was a friend he had to see. As he walked off through the entranceway he called out, "Don't run away."

"A lot of speechifying you been doing," Jake said. "You don't usually talk so much."

"It's the worry."

I thought how all the time, even when I was talking, I kept thinking about things that happened a long time ago. And thinking about Maddie and Jake and Annie and my life, like I was far away someplace or like maybe inside I knew I was never going to see any of it again.

"Quit that. Nobody knows, we may need all the energy we've got in a while. You just quit worrying and sit tight. Keep your eyes on me and if there's ever a chance for a break, I'll give you the sign."

"I just can't stop wondering."

"Well, try."

"I thought you said we couldn't break out of this one."

"Not yet. Later, when they take us out."

I thought: I should have tried to get away before they brought me here. At the time I never even thought of it, I couldn't think of anything except I'd been caught. Not till they closed the door.

Homer came back in with a friend, the same one I'd seen him with when they first brought me in. They sat down at the table in the center of the room and played dice again. They were talking in a language I didn't know the sound of, so I guessed it must be Greek. The friend spoke it slowly and let Homer correct him every now and then. In the middle of

39

the game Homer turned around and said, "You gamble?" Jake told him yes but he didn't always play it straight.

"Nobody else I gamble with does either, so it works out the same."

"I used to play," Homer said, "here, with men in the cells, but just pretend, no real money. One day a man's widow come to me and she swears her husband dying words was I owe him twenty-five thousand and she is to collect. You see, we play very high because is pretend. So now I don't do that no more."

The friend didn't do much talking. Just once he looked us both over and said to me, "You fight?"

I didn't understand.

"Fight. You fight ever, for money?"

"No," I said. "I don't like it. With the money or without. I figure why hurt people you don't even know."

"You got the build."

"Not me," I said, and pointed to Jake. "He's the one fights. He's been a boxer."

"I mean wrestling, that's the game. Too short in the legs to box. You'd be all right as a wrestler."

Jake was giving me a long, dirty look. The man said to him, "Where you box?"

"Oh, just here and there."

"Professional?"

"No, just amateur stuff."

"With the army?"

"Against the army."

"You know Big Quint? Old One-Punch Joe and the Sicilian Lion and Cassius what's-his-name?"

"I did," Jake said. "But a long time ago."

"And Killerboy Dexter? What a slugger that one was— and a fine left he had too, that fooled a lot of fighters. I suppose that was before your time. Best of the young ones coming up is that boy Rufus, comes from somewhere up North, some-place outside Syracuse, around there. Rufus—I forget his other name. I hear they're keeping him hid on a farm down in the country somewheres, training him with some of the oldtimers. Rumor is they're grooming him for the Olympics, but nobody admits to seeing him fight yet. Everybody just says he's the best coming up. A lot of money's started chang-ing hands on that boy. I'd bet myself if I could be sure. You hear anything on that score?"

"I wouldn't know anything about it," said Jake. "I haven't been around to the gym for a couple of years now."

"Wrestling's the game," the man said, and he went back to the dice.

It was hot. And it was getting darker. All the light came in from the entranceway and now that the sun was beginning to move, the place was almost in total darkness. Homer had brought a light in and put it on the table, and there were two more lamps up on the walls in front of the middle cells. But from where we were the light came dim and uneven and the place seemed cruder than before as the sun went. I began to long for air and the light that was still shining outside.

Another man came in suddenly and said something to Homer. The game broke up and all three went out.

"Listen," Jake whispered to me. "You're so nice and friendly today, but we all know already what a pal you are, so let's just have a little less of this exchanging birthday dates and how old people were when they got married and what's your great-grandmother's name and where you were when and what's your favorite color, right? And if you can't shut up about your own life-story, just at least leave mine out of it. What are you looking so pleased about?"

"I was just thinking about Homer and his wife. Shaped like a whale, with a name that means a green bough. That's nice."

"You goddamn fool," he said.

There was some shuffling around outside and a loud, firm voice I hadn't heard before. Homer's friend mumbled something and Homer began to talk, too. The big voice went on, lower and impossible to tell what it was saying. When he came back in Homer told us there'd been a big riot about two hours ago.

"Lots of arrest. Then there was two small riots in a different part of the town. Everybody say it look like she was plan like that, to take away attention and let the leaders escape. That's what they look for now because there are so many and you can't arrest allbody. Is bad, riots. Lots of people they don't even know there's riot going on, they just standing there doing nothing. Then the law bring them in to me, saying this is a dangerous criminal, and sometimes it's just girls and boys, so young and all beat up. Once I have a mother and child in the cells, very dangerous, they tell me. What they call—agitators, is it? Very dangerous agitators, this mother and child."

"How long do you keep them?" said Jake.

"Oh, that one, I mark it down and let them go, and lose the record later. That was on the other side of town, bigger jail and always full. Also I work with my friend, you see him? The one just leave. We have arrangements, you know."

"How'd we stand for an arrangement here?"

Homer looked over at the entranceway, rubbed his chin, and moved over to Jake's cell, right up near the bars.

"Here is different. I don't take the names, so I can't fix."

"But you got lots of friends in that department," Jake said. "Ain't that right?"

"Some, yes."

"I got friends too. What do you say to combining?"

"Not for theft," Homer says, and he pointed at Jake. "You, you do something. You know what the law is, but you do that anyway. I only fix it if people are here by mistake."

"It was a mistake. Mistaken identity. They mixed me up with somebody else. Some fool yelled stop that man, and I looked around, saw him going around the corner, and the law grabbed me instead. I tried to tell them at the time, but they were so all-fired happy to get their hands on anybody at all, they wouldn't listen."

"No?" said Homer. He didn't believe it.

"Truth," Jake said. "What do you say?"

He shook his head.

"No bad feeling, I do it if I believe is just. But is not so bad, you get out soon."

"Not soon enough. Look, Homer, you know how it is."

"Enough. Don't say no more, you make me angry. Sure, I know how it is. I always take what is coming to me. You do the same now. Is not so hard. I know how it is, so I know also what stories people tell the jailer and how you try to make sympathy and so on. See, I used to do it too, she's the first trick after telling the story to the law. All the things you say, I say them a long time ago."

"No harm trying," said Jake.

"Understand, I have sympathy, yes. What do I care? so they catch you, they take away what you try to take, so you don't profit. I think people should be charge money as punishment for theft. Charge them more money than the value of what they try to steal and give it to people they steal the thing from. You can't pay the charge, you can work it off. Then for small things, why make a thief stay in jail? Is not sensible. Because nobody is really hurt by it, not like hurting somebody's health or murder or other things. But that is personal opinion of mine, I don't let that change my mind. Is a question of law, you know. I know what is law.

You know what is, and you know before you come to my jail. And also, here it is more difficult than any other place I been. Very difficult. Other people are working here that I don't know. This place here, even if I think you are bad-treated when they bring you in, when they take you out, I cannot change it. Is my job, is my job to see you stay here till they have a trial. What else happpen is not my job. Beside, I could help at the beginning if you get arrested by the regular authority, but it was soldiers bring you in, isn't it? I got no friends high up there, up at the top where you need. Only with the local force I got friends high up. All I can do with the army is fix food and transportation and transfer, not take the name off the record."

I remembered what Jake said about how rickety the other jails were and how the best time to try for a break was when they took you out into the street.

"Could you get us transferred to a different place?" I said.

"Not now. All the jails is full now. But later, if they keep you here a long time, maybe."

"Thanks."

"No, no thanks. I only say maybe and if. It depends maybe on how many arrest they make with the riots and how they do the trial. Sometimes after riots they try all together in a block, get the jails clear quick, but sometime they wait and wonder who they got, specially if they think this riot was plan careful, not just a lot of people standing around. I see later if there's another place. But is too difficult, then I don't push. You understand is difficult for me without giving reasons why I change you. It use to be easy. I could do something even here, four, five month ago. Not now."

Jake asked him how long he expected they would keep us here.

"Hard to say. Maybe they keep you a long time here to wait for the trial. I hope is what they do."

44

"Like our company, do you?"

"Sure, sure, you and me we get along, right? I understand, you joke. Is not that. I mean, if they decide fast, give you a quick trial, it is with military trial and you get a harder sentence."

"But I was under civil arrest. I only met up with the military when they handed me over."

One of Homer's friends looked in at the doorway and said something. Homer turned around to answer him from where he stood.

Jake said, "Listen, Homer, if you would, there's something we'd both appreciate."

"Unlock. Yes, I bet."

"No, just if you could find out exactly how they've charged us, civil or martial law, and when they plan to try the cases."

"Sure, I do that anyhow. I always do that for my prisoner to save the worry."

"But don't lean too hard on the questions if it looks like some official's going to let it slide. I mean, if there's a holdup maybe I could get someone to change things from the outside, if you see what I mean."

"Sure," Homer said. "Is fair enough. Good luck to it. I cannot say exactly till the end of the day, maybe till tomorrow when they have gone over the day record. But I ask around, I find out what happen to your record, who got it, what they think happens to you. Meantime, I think you have company tonight—I hear there is some arrest to be transferred here, and maybe more people from riots, we see. Hope it don't mean you must double up. I keep saying to them it looks big but is small, only big walls is all."

"You're right there," said Jake.

He sat down on the floor. I'd been sitting on mine for some time, even though Jake had told me not to stay on the floor too long and not to sit totally still there because you'd lose the strength in your legs, and we might need it for a break later on. He kept moving back and forth and doing a kneebend up and down every once in a while. But I didn't believe any more it was going to be a question of getting out. Now I believed in the trial and didn't think it was going to be as bad as I'd imagined. I was feeling generally better about the future, except for what was going to happen to Maddie and the kids, and how she'd take it. If I was away for a long time, Annie could look after them. Jake always had plenty of money put by for when he was up against the law. But it couldn't turn out to be such a long time, not for just a piece of bread, I didn't think. I wasn't sure about the horse.

"Do you think they'll try us about the same time?" I asked him. "I wish it could be together. What's it like at the trials?"

He started to say something, but Homer came in again and sat at his table. People kept walking by and talking outside and the place seemed more open and lighter because now it was near sunset and the light was coming in on the slant. You could see it lying like patches of sand or like dust on the floor at the entranceway. Men came in, asking Homer things and going out again, talking to each other in the passageway. Then there was a commotion outside, a lot of voices and then stillness and right afterwards laughing and whistles and voices that seemed to be humming like water. Homer got up to see and went out the doorway. Jake stood up in his cell and then I did too.

"Another prisoner?" I said.

"A woman, bet you anything. Probably Annie."

Homer came back in sight. Annie was standing behind him, next to an officer who held her by the arm and grinned down at her. She said something to him, looking back into his face in a measuring sort of way, and almost smiled. He laughed and let go of her.

"I leave you to talk," Homer called, and waved his hand

46

towards us so she could see we were at the far end. Then he turned and motioned the other man to follow him out. Annie walked forward from between them, alone, across the center of the floor. She had her head up and walked easy, keeping her eyes on the side of the room where Jake was.

It was strange to watch how she was and know she didn't know I was there, or looking at her. Stranger than seeing somebody you know walk by in a crowd. She looked hard. Full of devilment, able to take care of herself, and ready to talk back. It made me almost shy, seeing her, the way she was when she wasn't at home and wasn't a sister—a woman coming to see her husband in jail, which was a thing she'd done lots of times before.

She sauntered up near the cell, flicked her eyes past me, lazy and sneery, and then looked. She stopped in the middle of walking so she nearly tripped, and her face changed.

"You? I thought it was Jake."

"Right behind you, honey," he said. She whipped around.

"You, oh you—this is the last straw. Lord, this is the limit. It's all right for you to go taking chances, but why you have to drag my kid brother into—"

"He didn't," I told her.

"This was one he done all by his own fool self," Jake said.

She turned around again and curled her fingers closed on the bars of my cell and leaned forward like she wanted to put her head through.

"Ain't you ashamed?" she said. "And what's Maddie going to do now you landed yourself in this place? Ain't you shamed?"

"No," I said, "I am not." I started to explain, but she didn't want to listen. All the time I was talking she was giving me her own talking-to. I couldn't listen to her and talk at the same time, and I suppose she couldn't have been listening to me either, for the same reason. But it didn't seem important.

47

At the time it only mattered that I was getting the explanation out.

"I was hungry," I said, "and I stole some bread. That's all there was to it. I was hungry enough so's I didn't bother much about who was going to be looking at me. That's all there is to it. I'm not ashamed, I'm just worried, sick with the worrying. And you don't make it any better. Do you think I like being here?"

"You should have thought. Oh my Lord, why didn't you come to me and say? You should be—"

"Cut it out, Annie," Jake said.

I said, "Listen, you'll tell Maddie, won't you? And tell her not to worry."

"Not to worry?"

"And see there's somebody can look after the kids for a while, so she can come and see me. I got to talk with her."

"I bet she'll enjoy that, walking through that line of studs out there and at night-time, too."

"How many out there?" Jake asked.

"About ten."

"Come over here, Annie."

She dropped her hands. They came away from the bars all at once as though they'd been stuck there instead of holding on. She went over to Jake and he put an arm through the bars and around her shoulders.

"They been giving you a hard time?"

"Just the usual, saying things. Asked me how much I cost."

"How much did you say?"

"Told them to ask my husband."

He put his other hand through and started to touch her face and neck. I had the feeling I shouldn't look and turned to the side, to the wall.

"Something I want you to do for me," he said. He began

to tell her names of people and where to go and what to say.

"Keep your eye on the entrance, will you, Seth?"

He started whispering something to her and she answered, and after a while sighed and said all right. Then he squeezed her to him against the bars and drew his arm back so it was just lying along her shoulder. She turned around and told me not to fret, that she'd see Maddie was all right and try to keep her from worrying. She looked tired.

"Somebody coming."

I could just see Homer's head moving into view and another man's hand, waving fingers in the air as he walked. Jake looked, too.

"What were you giving him the eye for?"

"Who?" she said.

"That tall number had you by the arm when you came in. Who is he?"

"How should I know? He was standing outside. Said he'd show me where you were."

"You have to play up to him like that?"

"I didn't play up to anybody. Anyway, who's talking? I bet you missed me last night, didn't you?"

"I missed you," he said. He was looking over her head at the other man and his face turned peaceful and set, getting angry.

"If I died," he said, "you'd get married again before the year was out, wouldn't you?"

She didn't move for a while. Then she lifted his hand, knocked his arm away, and walked back to the entrance without looking at either of us or saying goodbye. Jake leaned up against the side wall and ran his hand over the bars where she'd been.

"What are you looking at?" he said.

"Just looking."

He let go of the bars and turned his back.

I've seen it happen so many times before and every time it jars me up, because I don't understand how it can be. I've lost my temper with Maddie, hit her because I couldn't help it. But I never wanted to hurt her. And afterwards, knowing I'd hurt her, I felt as scared and miserable as if I'd killed her, so in the end she was the one who had to comfort me, though she was the one got hurt. With Jake and Annie it's different, they set out to hurt each other. That's what I can't understand about it, that they love as much as we do, and still they can plan out a hurt the way you would prepare a pleasure.

He's treated her so bad sometimes, not beating her around, but just saying something mean. She does the same. Both of them wild with the notion that the other one could be fooling around with somebody else. And all of it is uncalled for. I don't believe either one of them has stepped over the line since they got married. But they talk about it all the time, and threaten each other with it, and hint it might be so. At first I used to think it happened because they didn't have any kids, that they needed an extra thing to be in their marriage. But then I met up with other married people who were jealous that way, with two or three kids, and that just meant two or three more weapons in the battle as far as they were concerned.

Jake said to me once I was lucky I wasn't jealous. "I got no cause," I told him. "You don't either. So why be jealous," and he answered, "There don't have to be cause. You're born that way or born without it. Jealous means jealous from the start—possessive." Maybe that's what it is, that people just have different ideas about what belongs where. So if you are jealous that way, you imagine it should be possible that a body is yours when you have possessed it, and everything inside the body. I know he thinks that way about other things, like a horse or something like that belongs to the man that can take it, and if you can't hold on to what

50

you've got you don't deserve to have it. I don't hold with that—I don't approve. When I stole, I knew it belonged to somebody else. I knew it perfectly but I took it anyway. But for Jake, the horse was his as soon as he began to lead it away. Finders keepers is what he thinks about things, about objects.

But about people, how can you say that? I told him, the people you belong to, it's in your mind, in your soul. They could be a hundred miles away and living with somebody else but it would be the same inside you, wouldn't it? And you could belong to somebody who never belonged to you, who didn't give you a second thought, not even if you were married. "I'm not talking about love," he said, "just who she sees in the afternoons." I'd only be worried if Maddie didn't love me any more. As for anything else, I don't think it would happen, but if it did it wouldn't be the end. "You don't even have any cause, Jake," I told him. "And even if you did, you know where her heart is, so can't you stop treating each other like that?" He said, "A change of bed can cause a change of heart."

I couldn't get anywhere talking about it with him. Maddie used to talk to Annie too, after a quarrel, till we got dragged into it that time and I had to tell them. I told them both it was all right for them to get into these fights and come ask us to take sides, but in a week they'd be together again and meanwhile they'd have broke up our home so in the future they would have to settle it alone. Mostly it was just all the talk that went on, that's what I couldn't stand. Both of them, it's as if you could almost see them sewing or weaving with the words, as if they are ornamenting—a jab here, a stitch there, and it's obvious they enjoy it, but it makes my head ache. I figure if you think something, then say it and don't take all day over it, but if you aren't sure what you think, shut up till you've made up your mind.

Jake can talk. Like anything. I think he used to make up his mind while he was talking. It's not so much like that now, he's quieter now. But at the wedding when he came with Annie, Maddie's mother said, "Can he talk? That boy could steal the brains right out of your head with his talk." Now he keeps a lot to himself because of politics, and you don't know all he's thinking.

"Will you quit looking at me like that?" he said.

"Just looking."

"She'll get over it. It don't mean a thing. Just keep her so mad she won't have time to think about anybody else till I get out."

I said, "You know if anything happened to you she'd kill herself."

"Maybe."

"You know she would. Maddie's the one would get married again."

"You think so?"

I'd never thought about it before but now it seemed like I'd known all the time.

"Sure, and I'd want her to. If anything happened to her, I'd get married to somebody else again too. Not right away, but I would. I couldn't live alone like that. And neither could she. It would be worse for her—I'd want her to get married again. How'd she live with two kids and no man in the house? It's bad enough you'd have the grief, why should she be unhappy too?"

"You wouldn't be jealous?"

"What do you mean, jealous? I'd be dead. But I'd like to know she's all right. I'd like her to get married again to somebody would make her happy."

"You mean you'd want her to love some other man? Really, like she loves you now?"

"Yes, I would. After I'm dead." I wouldn't want to leave somebody and have the world turn black and be dead to them whenever they think of me not being there. Much better if they think of me kindly and know I want them to be happy. For the children, too. Isn't that love?

Jake said, "Well, you don't know what it is. My, I feel like I'd be jealous even after I was dead."

"That's why she wouldn't be able to go on afterwards," I told him. "You wouldn't either. Think about it. What would you do if anything happened to Annie?"

"I don't want to think about it. I don't know."

Homer came in with his keys and began to unlock one of the middle cells.

"She is pretty, very," he said. "Lots of what you call it? Temperament. We got girls like that at home."

"You got everything back there," Jake said.

"Sure. I have a cousin like that a long time ago. You say something and her eyes flash and she tell you to go to hell. Then she wait till everybody leave her alone and she cries, cry like she will die. Is pride, is wonderful in a woman."

"You know all about that too?" Jake said.

"Two years ago, three years ago—well. Now I am feeling old. Is the job, maybe." He went over to the other middle cell and unlocked that one too so the doors stood open.

Jake said, "Is there anything you don't have over there in Greece? By my count you invented poetry, politics, philosophy, women. What else is there you don't have?"

"Money," Homer said.

"How about religion, did you start that too?"

"You very religious?"

Jake laughed. I heard shouts out in the passage and stamping feet and a roar of people coming closer. And then an

53

armed guard burst through the entranceway, about seven of them, and they were dragging eight or nine people with them.

"Five in here," Homer said, and stood back. "Rest over there."

The soldiers began to cram them into the cells. They were young kids, looking not more than nineteen or twenty and two of them girls. All of them were kicking and hitting at the military and calling them paid tools of the government and hired butchers of imperialist tyranny and things like that. Then they started shouting names and dirty words, the girls too. But they must have come from good families; they were rich, you could see that. Most of the boys, about five of them, were dressed like me, dressed to look like a poor man, a fieldworker. But if you looked you could see their poor man's clothes were made out of real quality stuff.

The doors shut and they quieted down just for a moment. That's the bad time, when the door closes and you know there's no choice any more. But then they decided to put up a good front, and they yelled even louder than before, calling Homer names and jeering at him. I could see five of them, four boys and a girl. And if I got down into the corner I could see the other four on my side of the wall. But I didn't like the feeling of having those five all able to look straight into my cell with nothing I could do about it except turn my back. I got into the other corner and stood sideways so I could turn around whenever I wanted to, and watched them.

Homer waited for them to get quieter and then he and the friend he'd been playing dice with, the one who liked wrestling matches, started to hand in water and pots and things. One of the boys got his arm through the bars and poked the wrestling man hard in the eye. He grabbed the arm and twisted it and I heard a snap. "You've broken my arm," the boy yelled, "my God, he's broken my arm!"

54

The girl in the cell started to scream: "You dirty bastard, you filthy motherfucking son of a bitch." The ones in the other cell were shouting, "Police brutality, imperialist pig," and then all of them smashed the pots against the bars and the walls and threw the water out over the floor and began to throw the broken pieces into the center at Homer and his friend. There was water and smashed pieces everywhere, and they begin to sing. One of the freedom songs, one of ours.

Homer stood by the table and put his hand to his friend's face, looking at the eye. Then he took him by the arm and they both walked out, leaving everything on the floor. The singing went on.

When they'd finished there was a silence. The reaction's coming, I thought. "Hey, how's your arm?" one of them said from the other side. I moved over and looked out to the side and could see him with his face against the bars. I thought he must be the leader; he'd started the song. He had a little beard and a sunburn. I imagined he must have worked hard for both of them. The others were all very white from sitting up late at night talking about politics. Jake says I should be aware of what's going on but he didn't appear to be too set on them either. I looked over and saw him yawn and do another kneebend.

Back in the cell I could see, one of the boys said, "What a filthy place. I've got to pee." "Go ahead," one of the others told him, "give them some work to do for all the money they're getting beating people up." The girl and some of the others began to giggle. "Me too," said another boy and then they both did it against the wall while the rest cheered. After that they were quiet for a while. I could smell it coming through the place, a hot vegetable smell, going sour. There seemed to be less air than before.

A couple of them sighed and mumbled to each other. One of the boys said, "Well, what are we going to do to fill in the time?" and put his arm around the girl. I supposed she was his girl because she let him and they began to kiss up against the bars. One of the boys looked embarrassed and turned away, but the others looked on while they kissed. Then they began to do more, he started to undo her clothes, and I thought: Lord, they're going to, right where everybody can see. But the girl appeared to be bored and pushed him away. "I'm not in the mood," she said. He nuzzled up to her again and said, "Come on, you're always in the mood, aren't you?" She took his arms away and said, "Cut it out," and moved away from him, one elbow out with her hand on her waist and holding onto the bars with the other hand. She tossed her hair back from over her eyes and stayed like that. I saw her face; she was still trying to look bored. And I thought: that one's just lost her forever, and it's a good thing. That's what they come to jail for, to get right down to real life, to the truth, and if you're looking for it there, that's where you'll find it.

Someone was crying outside in the passage. Everybody looked. "Beating up some poor kid," one of them said, and the crying went on. Homer and his friend came around the corner of the passage and out through the entrance, supporting a man between them. He was one of us, and he was still crying and had trouble standing. But he wasn't hurt, I didn't think. It must have been grief. Because he was crying the way people do when it's all over, and everything around you disappears so you can't even see what you're looking at and you don't care any more. They put him in one of the big cells, the one to the right of the entrance, and closed the door. Homer said something to him but the man couldn't answer. He sat down on the floor and kept on crying, running his hands over his head and face and not even bothering to turn awa $\iota$.

One of the kids called out, "What did you do to him? Are

56

you proud of that? What did you do to that man?" Homer didn't look around. He went back outside with his friend and came in again alone and began to clean up the floor. The kids said things to him, trying to get his temper, but he kept on cleaning, not looking at them and his face resigned, not grim like I would be. When he finished, he stood up, holding all the broken pieces.

He said to them, "There is three men outside, your fathers or your uncles or something. They pay to get you out. They also pay for destruction of government property, for this. Men come in here and I try to make it clean as possible because it is bad enough to be in jail without the discomfort. You think I got lots of these? You think with all things going on so fast the state has time to give me supplies? No, I buy things myself and I keep the place clean myself and if I don't, there come diseases. Now you go piss on the wall and what happens if twenty more people come here and no time to clean it up? You do not think of other people who come after you, they have to live with all the things you break and make dirty."

"That's tough," one of them said. "You're making me cry." And another one said, "That's what you're paid for, isn't it?"

"I am pay by your fathers and uncles and the rest. They are rich and they treat me all right. When you have money, twenty years from now, you will pay me. But you will treat me like dirt. That is the difference," he said, and went out. The man in the front cell kept sobbing and I began to feel bad and tired from all the noise. I sat down on the floor.

"Hey," one of them called. He was in the cell on my side. I thought it was the voice of the tanned one with the beard. He was calling to Jake. "What are you in for, brother?"

"Brother, hell," Jake said. "I never seen you before in my life."

57

"We're on your side," the voice explained. Jake didn't answer, and the voice said again, "What are you in for?"

"Child rape," Jake said. A few of them laughed, and then it sounded like the laugh was dying out and they weren't sure, because his face hadn't changed.

"You're kidding," the voice said.

"No," Jake told him, and turned away.

"How about you?" another boy said from the cell that looked into mine. "What are you in for?" He smiled and I had that feeling that we were tied together, like when somebody you don't like smiles and it's as if you're standing at the other end of the line, his smile jerks up one on you, and you don't want it to happen, it makes you mad that it might respond all by itself, because you don't like the person. I thought against it so my face didn't move and I didn't answer him, and turned my head to the wall like Jake.

The man at the far end kept on sobbing. Some more of the kids tried to speak to us but I wasn't playing. Neither would Jake, which surprised me. He knows all their ideas and the language they use. I don't understand it and I'm damned if anybody is going to do that charity thing to me: we are sorry for you, we sympathize, we're fighting for your betterment, stand here like a monkey and look pleased and think how good we are. Or they give you food and clothes which you're not in a position to refuse, and when they leave they've robbed you of your honesty, your smile tied to the one they have that says: aren't you grateful, don't you like us, isn't it a lucky thing for you that we think about you once a year. They get very uncomfortable and vexed and sometimes scared if they think you're laughing at them behind their backs, and then they don't come back the next year and your kids have to do without, like you.

I heard Homer's voice and a lot of steps coming in. The military was back. "They buy you out," Homer says, and began to unlock the cells. One of the kids said they hadn't asked anybody to buy them out and they were going to stay there as a protest against police brutality. The soldiers began hauling them out. The one with the hurt arm came out quiet enough, wanting to get to a doctor. Some of the others put up a fuss. The girl from the other side suddenly kicked one of the guards for no reason at all, it looked like. He swore and let go and she kicked him again. His friend who was standing next to them pulled back his fist and hit her in the breast. She screamed all the way out and was crying and saying, "You coward, you dirty coward."

Then they were out in the passage, the sound of them going, and it was quiet except for the man who was weeping.

"Did you see that?" Jake said. "Got him on the shinbone twice before they ever thought of laying a hand on her, and she'll go home and show her bruise and tell how she was roughed around by the hired imperialist thugs who've got nothing better to do all day than beat up women and kids."

"I thought you liked those kind of people, protest and rights and all."

"Not from them, it's too late for it now. It was a nice gesture, very helpful in the beginning, but we don't need them any more, they're just in the way. Besides, it's a kind of mental slumming for most of them. We want them out in the streets when they're landowners and senators and running import-export businesses like their folks, when they've got the pull to change the laws, change everything. But I bet, I bet you anything, in twenty years when they've got the family holdings and the house and everything, they'll be taking their kids on vacations to a little villa outside Rome or someplace and voting themselves tax reductions so they can keep what they got. And once in a while they'll boast to the kids about how they went through that stage too, they were idealists and right in the middle of the violence, where the action was."

59

"Singing our songs," he went on. "They've got songs of their own—why don't they work on that? They take it from us and they'll drop it in a few years. Retain the sympathy, of course, a lot of good that does."

"You're always saying people should fight for their rights."

"Sure, sure. If you know what they are and know what you're doing. I'm just sick of all this idealism running around the place. It's like an epidemic, everybody's got it. Trouble with idealism is it kills people. I'm not interested in motives, I just want something that works out without too much strain on everybody. Man, you talk with some of the people I know. Fanatics. Got a lot of schemes but what's in their minds is that they want to take over the show. Just the system all over again, we'll get on top and then we'll stomp on you for a change. And the people who've really got something to cry about, can you move them? Hell no. If there's a takeover they'll still be at the bottom. And all the ones that complain and won't lift a finger, think if everything was distributed equal nobody'd ever have to work again—I'm sick of all of it."

"Well, they wouldn't. Have to work again."

"You're crazy."

"Not what I call work, not what I been doing for the last nine years every day."

"That ain't work, that's slaving."

Homer came in again and started to clean out the floor of the cell and scrub the walls.

"What about them?" he said. "Did you hear the things that girl was saying? If that's my daughter I throw her out of the house and never come back, you bet."

The weeping man calmed down a little and started to moan. Every once in a while he'd break into sobbing again, but it was quieter. He had his head down on his knees and his arms around them.

"What's his trouble?" Jake asked.

Homer came over and said in a low voice that the man had stabbed his wife.

"Dead?"

"Instant, just like that. The neighbors say they quarrel all the time, shout. He never beat her, maybe he should. This time they shout at each other across the table and there's a knife there on top. He says he don't mean to hurt, all he mean was to shut up the shouting so she would listen. He is heart-breaking, he loves her very much. The neighbors say is true what he says, no other man, no other woman, just being angry. Very sad. They will try it as accidental I hope. He says he wants the trial right now, wants to die."

"Poor bastard, poor fool," Jake said.

Homer went back to scrubbing down the cells. I had to use the pot and then I thought I'd sleep. All day I usually move around, I never knew how tired you get if you stay shut in. And I was feeling the bruises and beginning to stiffen up from when they pushed me around making the arrest. They can tell who's rich and who isn't and who's got friends. They never roughed Jake around unless he got in first. He looks too smart and too important.

I stretched. Homer began to whistle and to hum. I lay down on the floor and put my head on the stone, cold and hard. Then I changed around and put my arm under my head and closed my eyes.

I must have gone right under. When I woke up a man I'd never seen before was talking in whispers to Jake, saying goodbye. I sat up and watched him leave and saw Annie at the entrance, going out with him into the dark hallway.

"How long was I out?" I said.

61

"Not very long. She says Maddie's coming later. Uncle Ben will walk her here, and Annie's going to look after the kids."

"She still mad at you?"

"No," he said, "no, we made it up," and smiled.

"Good."

The man who'd killed his wife was still sobbing quietly. "Has he been at it all this time?"

"No, he let up for a time. He only started again a little while back. Homer says they're moving him on later."

"I hope we don't get any more rioters."

"So does Homer. It cuts down on the food."

"That's funny, you know, I thought it would make me feel sick. I did feel sort of unsettled, but not sick. And I'm hungry again. Already."

"It's the idea. Watch out for that. You know in your mind you'd like to keep on eating all day long. But your stomach can't take it. So take it slow."

"Is there any news?"

"Not much. Not good. I got Joe to hunt out my army friends."

"Virgil?"

"Him and others. They don't know anything, don't know where to begin. I never knew such a total breakdown of grapevines. We'll just have to sit it out till something comes through."

Homer came in and unlocked the other cell by the entrance, the big one on the left.

"Another noisy one," he said. "I put him far away as possible." While he was speaking four guards came in with the prisoner, squirming and writhing in his clothes like an animal in a sack, and muttering to himself. He was the strangest looking thing: all gawky, skinny as a reed and dressed in rags that were covered in dirt. His hair fell all over his eyes and below his shoulders and even from a distance I thought I could see things hopping off him. He stuck out one long bony leg while they tried to move him along, and you could see the toenails on his bare feet, longer than I imagined nails could grow, like the nails on his hands, black with dirt. And there were sores on his legs, which were the color he was all over, a kind of livery yellow.

"Blasphemers," he blared out in a voice like a trumpet call, but it made you want to laugh. Then it broke, and he trilled what he was saying in a high quavering voice that sounded as if it was coming from a completely different person.

"Repent, the day is at hand. Oh ye ungodly, ye of little faith." He screwed his head around and I stepped back farther into the cell. His face gave me the kind of sinking feeling you get when you see blood, but that kind of fascination, too. I'd never seen anybody like that, so that you felt revolted but you couldn't take your eyes off him. They say snakes do it to birds.

"Goddamn, we've got the whole works now," Jake said. "A week in this jail and you could write a history of the world."

"Unrighteous and ungodly," said the stranger. "Pharisees, Pharisees!"

He had great blazing eyes and inside his beard a loose mouth full of rotten teeth. When he called out "Pharisees" the eyes rolled up and his face went all meek and mockpious, so for a moment I was sure he was putting on an act for some reason.

They shut him in the cell and Homer turned the key and stood back, brushing off his clothes. The stranger rattled the bars and sang out, "Eaters of offal, ye that persist in the ways of the ungodly, Pharisees!" He went on like that, his eyes roaming over the rest of the cells for a while, but none of us gave him a reaction, so he turned around and sat down with his back leaning against the bars, and scratched his head and muttered to himself.

"What kind of a thing is that?"

"Some religious nut," Jake said. "Some kind of faith-healer probably."

"Why's he in here? He looks sick."

"Maybe he was preaching to the multitudes or something when the riots broke out. Start screaming and kicking enough and they pull you in. Some of them do it for the food and a a place to sleep for the night."

Homer came up to Jake, who said to him, "I got a complaint to register about the way the tone of this place is going down. It's turning into a regular sideshow. What's the world coming to when a man can't find any peace and quiet even in jail?"

"You tell me?" Homer said. "You tell me. Food is soon."

"And drink?"

"Sure, drink too. Coming soon," he said, and went out.

"I could do with a drink," Jake said.

Lots of things I could do with, I thought. The air was still heavy and thick and the place had the sense of something wild having passed through and gone, time coming back and sitting there slow. I was thinking I hoped they'd put me out to do hard labor because I couldn't take a lot of this, being shut in. Maybe you got used to it, though. I planned the first thing I'd do when I found out how long the sentence was going to be. It would be to do what all the others do, so they tell you: find someplace where I could mark off the days one by one.

"Goes by slow when you got to wait it out," I said. "I wish we knew one way or the other right now without a trial, what the sentence is."

"I know right now. I know they aren't going to keep me in

for long. Not if I can help it. I been sentenced three times and never yet served one. Don't let yourself slide back that way. Do you want to be cut off from the world for the next ten years?"

"Ten years for a piece of bread?"

"Lord, Seth. Don't you know anything?"

That's what he always said when we were kids. Nobody would believe he was older because he was so small, it took a long while before he got his growth. Maybe that's why he likes to fight, because he's never forgotten how he used to have to. "Don't you know anything?" he'd say, and pretty soon they weren't laughing any more, everybody was taking orders from him.

"Don't you know anything? You don't imagine they're going to go easy on you because you give them some hard-luck story, do you?"

"For taking a piece of bread? What do you think they're going to do, cut my hand off or something? They couldn't give me more than six months, could they? I never stole anything before."

"So you say. But wait till you hear what they say. Wait till some man stands up and says, yes that's the one that burned down my business last year, and some woman says she's positive you're the one raped her grand-daughter just a week ago, she remembers your shifty eyes, and swearing up and down on oath and a dozen witnesses to prove it. Asking you where you were on such-and-such a night three years ago and looking triumphant when you say you can't remember. Don't you know that? If every man was just charged with the crime he's done, everybody there is would be in jail for something. Hell no, you get arrested and you're a representative for all the ones who never got caught out."

I thought it couldn't be like he said, he was trying to scare me about it. Maybe he figured if I got too relaxed I'd drop some hint about his political doings. I wasn't all that relaxed; my hands were sweating again.

Homer and the four-man guard came in with the food. First they went to the cell on the right, where the man was moaning to himself about his dead wife. He didn't raise his head from his knees or move in any other way. Homer gave his keys to one of the others, went into the cell himself, and laid the provisions down on the floor while the ex-fighter stood behind him. He locked up again and the man still didn't move. Then they went over to the left-hand cell and started to open up. The religious nut jumped to his feet and began chuckling to himself. "Stand back, there," one of the guards said and he moved a little way back, but he kept pacing back and forth, making noises to himself like he was agreeing with something someone was saying to him, and holding his arms out with the fingers bent like claws.

Homer went into the cell and was about to set the food down when the religious nut made a dash at him, knocking everything out of his hands and sending it way up into the air. The food and drink and water splashed all over the inside of the cell and on the walls and over Homer and the guard by the door. The nut shrieked out, "Get thee behind me, get thee behind me, spawn of the devil," and began to dance around the cell. The ex-professional stepped forward and cracked him across the mouth. And he let out a yelp, not sounding like pain, sounding like some kind of a love-sound a woman might make. They closed the doors on him and Homer went out into the entranceway with the fighter, leaving the other three men behind. The religious nut capered around his cell and began to harangue them, saying, "Man shall not live by bread alone but by every word that proceedeth out of the mouth of God." His voice kept changing, sometimes loud and strong as a whip cracking and then going all quavery and high and his face would turn back to

66

that mealy-mouthed humble look. When he said "mouth of God" he lifted his right hand and pointed his finger up at the ceiling, throwing his eyes up dramatically.

He went on parading in front of them, stalking back and forth and shouting out a long string of stuff at them. He said, "I am the living bread, the living bread which came down from heaven, and if any man eat of this bread he shall live, he shall live, live forever. And the bread that I will give, the bread, the bread that I will give is my flesh. My flesh which I give, my flesh which I give, give for the life of the world."

"I know what's wrong with him, all right," one of them said. "Is that your trouble, sweetheart?" He laughed.

A second one said, "God, it makes you sick, look at him."

The religious nut was panting with excitement and his mouth was wet.

"I knew a nut like that once," the second one said, "went around hammering nails into his hands. It's a sex thing, gives them some kind of a kick. They run around shouting at people till somebody beats them up—that's what they want. Did you hear him squeal just then? Loves it."

The third guard, a good-looking boy and younger than the others, said, "You shouldn't laugh at crazy people."

"What's eating you?" the first one said. "You got religion all of a sudden?"

"I just don't think it's funny, that's all. They can't help it. Some of the things they say aren't so crazy—they're just like everybody else, only it comes out scrambled. He's not hurting anybody, is he? Everybody's a little crazy, every religion's a little crazy."

"Not everybody," the second one said. And not every religion. Is that what you meant to say, *every* religion is crazy?"

The younger one shrugged, and said he just didn't think it was funny and besides it was unlucky to laugh at crazy people.

"Crazy? Why, he's a goddamn raving pervert," the first one said.

The religious nut kept muttering all the time they were talking about him. As soon as they stopped he got their attention again and said, "The hour is coming, the hour is coming when the dead shall hear the voice of the son of God. I am the son and he that honoreth not the son honoreth not the father that sent him. The hour is coming. I am the son of God, I am the son of God. As soon as they hear of me they shall obey me, the strangers shall submit themselves unto me."

"What did I tell you?" said the first guard.

"It is God that avengeth me and subdueth the people under me. He beat them small as the dust before the wind, he cast them out like the dirt in the streets."

"Who are you calling dirt, you bastard?" the second guard said to him, and started to put his arm through the bars.

Homer came back in with the other one and said sharply, "What you doing making him shout like that? Come on, this is time for working. What you think, you can stand there all day? The food is getting cold." He shooed them into the passageway and came over to us, not looking at the religious nut who was still mumbling and shouting and hopping up and down. He shouted, "I receive not honor from men. Blessed are they that hear the word of God, but I know you, that ye have not the love of God in you. I am come in my father's name and ye receive me not."

"I'd like to receive him," I said. "Right in the teeth, I'd like to."

Homer said, "This day is the longest day in my life, I bet. First one thing, then another. Why they get him started like that? And I got to clean that up too. And now the other one start to cry again, no wonder. Oh, I am feeling old as one hundred today. And there is more people coming tonight. When I sleep I don't know."

"Who is he anyway?" Jake said. "What's he in for? Exposing himself to little girls, or what?"

"Is a mistake, all a mistake. I don't know why they send him here. He is sick and crazy. This is a jail, not a place for sick peoples. I ask his name to put it on the record and he just keep saying: I am the son of God. Like that, in a big echo voice and turn his eyes up. What he is arrest for I don't know because nobody send the charge record and he is transferred from someplace else. What a mess in my jail all day."

"Try a little of that Greek philosophy," Jake said.

"My philosophy for today is this," Homer says, and made a gesture with his hand.

Jake laughed. "Is that Greek, too?"

"Is international, yes?"

The food came in with the four guards, first to Jake's cell, next to mine, and then they all went out. I had some of the drink first and felt better. That man was crying again but the other one had stopped, and I began to eat.

Suddenly he started up again in that high, quivery cooing voice.

"I know you, that ye have not the love of God in you," he said. "I am come in my father's name and ye receive me not. My God, my God, why hast thou forsaken me, why art thou so far from helping me and from the words of my roaring? Oh my God, I cry in the daytime but thou hearest not, and in the night season, and am not silent. But thou art holy, oh thou that inhabitest the praises of Israel. Our fathers trusted in thee, they trusted, and thou didst deliver them. They cried unto thee and were delivered, they trusted in thee and were not confounded."

I began to feel let down and sad again. The noise kept going on, sometimes soft and sweet and sometimes bleating out strong and showing off. The soft voice was the worst, it made you feel crawly inside.

"But I am a worm and no man," he went on. "A reproach of men and despised of the people. All they that see me laugh me to scorn, they shoot out the lip, they shake the head, saying: he trusted on the Lord that he would deliver him— let him deliver him, seeing he delighted in him. But thou art he that took me out of the womb, thou didst make me hope when I was upon my mother's breasts. I was cast upon thee from the womb, thou art my God from my mother's belly. Be not far from me, for trouble is near, for there is none to help."

I turned around in the cell and put my back to the bars, feeling terrible all of a sudden and wanting to cry. I thought: if that man who killed his wife starts up again I won't be able to hold it back.

The voice went on: "Many bulls have compassed me, strong bulls of Bashan have beset me round, they gaped upon me with their mouths as a ravening and roaring lion. I am poured out like water and all my bones are out of joint. My heart is like wax, it is melted in the midst of my bowels, my strength is dried up like a potsherd. And my tongue cleaveth to my jaws, and thou hast brought me into the dust of death. For dogs have compassed me, the assembly of the wicked have inclosed me, they pierced my hands and my feet. I may tell all my bones, they look and stare upon me. They part my garments among them and cast lots upon my vesture. But be not thou far from me, oh Lord, oh my strength. Haste thee to help me."

"Seth?" Jake said, and I turned around. "Not hungry?"

"It's that goddamn nut. That awful mealy-mouth voice and the words so beautiful. What is all that stuff he's been spouting?"

"That? That one's a paslm. He's praying. The rest of it he's grabbed from all over the place, quoting from lots of different parts of the scriptures and getting them all mixed up."

"It's that voice, that awful voice. Can't they shut him up?"

"He'll stop it if you leave him alone. He wants an audience, that is all."

"I can't stand him," I said. "I hate him."

"Shouldn't hate."

"Why not? I'm beginning to think there's lots of things I hate. Never had time to think about them before."

"It's bad for the digestion," he said. "Besides, you hate somebody, that means they got a hold over you. They got you right in their hand."

"I don't see it. What is that, religious morality? All they tell you about in religion, it's full of hate. Hating all the ones that don't agree with you."

He began to tell me a story about a boy that lived next door before his family moved near us and we got to know each other. This boy took a dislike to Jake, a real hatred. One day the boy was making fun of him and Jake turned around and told him he wished he'd die. Next week the boy hung himself. I didn't believe it.

"It's true," he said.

"I mean I don't believe he would do it just because you said that."

"Lots of things people do. Specially when they build up hate like that and don't know how to get rid of it. If you're going to hate you should know why and what it is and how to keep it in control. Otherwise it can turn around and fall back on you. Why do you think you hate him?"

The voice had stopped now and I felt easier.

"I just can't abide his sicky-sweet psalmsinging voice. I don't mind so much that he's a nut."

"What's wrong with the voice?"

"Gives me the cold shakes," I said. I began to eat, to feel filled with the taste of it, and it was much better and I thought about seeing Maddie soon.

71

Jake sighed. He said, "A brother-in-law that's got the cold shakes, a weepy homicide case, a religious maniac who thinks he's the Messiah and a jailer who's a Greek philosopher—Lord, do I pick them."

"Do you remember when you were religious?" I said.

"A long time ago, that was."

I remembered. I remembered he even thought he had a calling and would go into it for life. Some of them are like that. They say a reformed sinner makes the best man of God because he can know and understand other people's weaknesses and help them to peace the way he found it. And it works the other way, too—the ones who brood about religion suddenly throwing it over and going wild, like Jake, and they never go back to it. When they change like that it's lifelong. Not like me. All my life I could never make up my mind about those things and in the end I realized I never would. I remember Jake would say, "There's got to be something more, there must be. Sometimes I feel like it's all a reflection or like a shadow of the real thing," and to listen to him talk about the mystery of things, you'd get all calm and serene and inside you were burning with the knowledge that everything was completely mysterious and large and full of unthought-of marvels. But I never felt that way by myself. It took Jake talking about religion to make it happen.

Then he changed. Once he said maybe God was just the way things happened, that everything that took place, all put together, made God. He said how he'd always wanted to experience what the scriptures spoke about: that God would talk to you. But that would mean God was a person and acted like a person, and if he was perfect and all-powerful he wouldn't be a person, because people are so small. Not just that they die, they're all-over small. All the believers who tell you you're doing something wrong or a thing or an action of yours is immoral because God wants this and God wants that; Jake said this God that's talking to them, that's themselves. That's their idea of what their good selves are like and what they'd wish to have happening in the world.

Then he got stuck on ideas. And he said religion was ideas but he wanted ideas that could handle people in this world, not deal with some world after death, which he'd never really taken to heart anyway. He began to get interested in politics. And he told me, like telling me I was lucky not to be jealous, "You're lucky you've got that instinctive certainty of what's right and what's wrong. I never had it." And by that he meant that I wasn't as smart, since I'd never gone into the question deep enough to find out that there's no such thing as right or wrong. Just how you happen to look at it, which was another thing he told me. I knew he was smarter, but some things he didn't see, for instance that I'd know when he said I was lucky to be this or that, that it was a way of telling me I had a place and it was just a notch below his. Some of the mistakes he makes with people—that's why, because he could misjudge those instinctive certainties. Not so much with strangers, there he was always all right.

And he made friends in the army and got them to give him information about where certain troops were stationed and what manoeuvres they were carrying out, how long they'd be staying, how the communication lines were set up, and so on. Passing it on to freedom fighters and the protesters, I suppose, and I'm sure, I know, there's a name for that and a very special law that covers it, overthrowing the state and all. They've got his name in one place and his description in another, and nobody's put the two together so far, but Maddie says she wouldn't be in Annie's place for anything in this world.

One day he says to me, "Maybe you're right about it all being in the mind, who you belong to. That's the thing, to possess minds, to be able to influence people, make them change their minds and change their lives. That's the real power, to get other men's minds under your control." So that's what he does now, and I still don't understand and maybe never will. What on earth would you want with somebody else's mind? Bad enough you're stuck with your own.

"Thou didst make me hope when I was upon my mother's breasts," Jake said, "that just tears my insides out. I think that's what I liked most about it, just the words."

"You called me Seth," I said.

"Nobody to hear. Don't you start doing it or you'll trip up."

They came back and opened up to take the things away. I was feeling a little drunk, though it was hard to tell, sitting down. They'd given us more this time. When they went to the religious nut's cell and cleaned it up he began jabbering again and after they'd locked up he made a grab at one of them through the bars. Homer wasn't with them this time, he'd given the keys to his wrestling friend and you could see his eye was already swelled out a lot from where the protester had hit him. At the cell on the other side they took out the food but left everything else. And then they went out again.

Homer came back with a new set of guards, the night shift, I guessed. They had about six people in tow and put them into the side cells where the kids had been. They were all working men, most of them looking pretty much like me, and very beat up, looking tired and dazed and not talking or trying to push back. The religious nut quoted a lot to them but they took no notice. Two of them lay down on the floor. Homer and the guards handed in water and something to to drink and pots, and came back later with food but not as much as they'd given us.

While they were eating the religious nut's speech dribbled off into muttering, then he quit entirely and sat down with his back to the bars. Homer came across the center of the floor, around the table, and said to me, "Is Maddie, yes?"

"Yes," I said and stood up. My heart started going all the way up through me and I hung onto the bars. He walked her across the room from the entranceway towards my cell and then went out, leaving us to talk. She looked shy and scared coming across the floor with all the men in the place.

When she got to the cell she put her arms through and up around my shoulders. All the hard work she does, and her hands so small. I put my arms through and held her close up to the bars and wanted to get my head through.

"Are you all right?" she said. "Are they feeding you all right?"

"I'm fine. Don't worry about me. I'm sorry, I'm sorry about all of it, Maddie. But you get Annie to stay with you and don't worry about me. It's you I'm worrying over, everything else is all right."

"Ben and Mary asked about you," she said. "Annie told them you'd gone to visit her cousin Liza, so I had to back her up. I didn't know you had a cousin Liza."

I had to laugh because cousin Liza was a family joke and a name to use for excuses when you wanted to get out of something. I was never sure we really had any cousin by that name; Annie knew more about those far-off cousins than I ever did. I remembered she once told me cousin Liza had been a notorious old woman who disgraced the family at some point and died about forty years ago.

I told Maddie and she relaxed a little and didn't look so strange. She gets that pinched-up look sometimes like she's a very old woman, and when she looks that way she also appears to be about four years old, all the ages come into her face.

Jake said hello, and she said hello to him and turned back

to me. I wished there weren't any other people around, so I could really talk. It felt shaming to be overlooked by so many people and not able to speak really. I thought: this must be the worst part of being in jail for a long time—standing near the people you love but not quite able to touch them and not quite able to talk to them and sweating with the constraint; counting, all the time they are there, how much more time there is until they've got to go. So much to say, and unable to.

"Well," Maddie said. "Well, I'll look in tomorrow."

Just then the religious nut threw himself against the bars of his cell and pointed his finger at us, and bellowed out, "Daughter of Sodom, Jezebel, beware the sins of the flesh, beware!"

Maddie looked behind her and I looked, over her head, seeing him writhing himself up against the bars, moving in a jerky rhythm and roaring, "Beware the unclean lusts of the flesh, beware the guile of painted women that leadeth unto temptation! My judgment is just because I seek not mine own will but the will of the father which hath sent me."

I tasted the food coming back up my throat and felt Maddie in trembles between my hands, like from cold, and I couldn't take it any longer.

"Shut up," I yelled, "shut that goddamn bastard up, shut him up, Homer, make him quit!" And then it happened again like I always try to avoid, like a curtain of blazing light coming down over my forehead, getting mad and not knowing or caring any more, not hearing what anybody else was saying, just yelling that I was going to kill him when I got my hands on him.

Then I heard Jake, quiet, saying, "Easy, take it easy. You're making it worse."

I looked up and saw his face and felt the hotness begin to go and the shaking come on.

76

"That's just what he wants," he said. "Take a look. It's you he's interested in, not Maddie."

I looked and saw the nut with one foot through the bars now, weaving his body back and forth, and looking straight at me. His eyes were nasty and pleased, his mouth wide open and blood down the side of his face from where he'd been hit. Seeing me look, he started up again, started whipping himself into a frenzy, running his hands all over his body. But Jake got in first.

"Just don't listen," he said. "Now he knows he can get a rise out of you, he'll try it again."

I turned my head away and began to cry. Maddie smoothed her hand over my neck and said, "Oh Seth, oh Seth."

Homer came in then and said what was the trouble, what had happened.

'That crazy son of a bitch, insulting my wife."

Homer went over to his cell and the nut pulled his foot in and gave him a short lecture in his trumpet voice. Homer stood there without saying anything, and the nut slouched off into one of the far corners and sat down.

Maddie said, "Oh Seth, putting you in with horrible people like that."

I told her again not to worry, and touched her face and took her hand in through the bars and kissed that. She did the same with mine and Homer made a sign from the entranceway that it was time for her to go. She looked back as she went, and I thought: if that other one makes a remark or does anything at all, even coughs when she gets up close— But he didn't look at her and she went out with Homer.

Later in the night the guards came and took the homicide out of his cell. He'd stopped crying but he went with them blank-faced. I wondered if they were taking him to trial. Homer had quit work for the night. Before he went he'd

77

promised us to remember about looking up the day records. The man who took over was one I hadn't seen before, very thin and grey-haired and sullen. All night long they were changing men in the middle cells, taking out the ones who were there and replacing them with others. I didn't think they could be rioters, only a few of them looked like they'd been in a fight. The rest were all ordinary looking men, some young and some older. They tried to sleep when they came in, but hardly had time because the guards were moving them so fast. I guessed finally that they were all being held for questioning about something. Jake said he was going to sleep. Over by the entrance the religious nut was rolled up in a ball in a corner of his cell. I was tired, but it had been so dark in the place for so long that I didn't think I could sleep. I lay down and kept watching the people going in and out.

Finally I thought I would sleep after all and make myself a dream. Maddie said once she didn't dream, she said she supposed that meant she didn't have any imagination, and looked embarrassed. I told her all it means is that she forgets them when she wakes up. I'm always talking about them since it means a lot to me. Some people don't care about it or don't like the thought of dreaming, or are scared by it, by the thought that they go someplace away from the body. Jake says you don't, it only seems that way, like being able to remember a face, you can close your eyes and call it up by thinking, and you don't truly leave. Maybe Maddie has dreams she doesn't want to remember; I'd want to remember even the bad ones.

When we were kids we used to compare. Annie dreams in black and white and repeats dreams and remembers what people say in them. Jake's are in color, like mine, and people in them talk but you don't remember what they've said, only maybe a word once in a while. Same with mine. But

78

he dreams about people he knows and I don't usually unless they are far away. My little girl Mary is the strangest one —she's dreamed some things that have happened afterwards. She dreamed about the fire before it happened, and about Maddie's grandfather dying. Last week she said she had a dream about me, she dreamed I was in a big parade or some kind of celebration and we were all going somewhere to do something important. She said it scared her but afterwards she thought it must be all right because though she didn't see the end, the dream finished halfway, when I was in it I was looking happy.

I closed my eyes and tried for a good dream. I like planning them out just before you go under. Then they take over and change, of course, and the real dreaming begins.

When I woke up I didn't know where I was and then remembered and knew the dream had been a bad one. I'd had a feeling in the dream that I was all bent down and weak and couldn't move very well, and people I'd met a long time ago kept asking me what had happened to me. And the trouble was I was old, about a hundred years old with a long white beard. But I'd felt it in my body, withered up and broken and too feeble even to say what was wrong with me.

Jake looked like he was still asleep. The cell where the weeping man had been now had about six men in it, all asleep on the floor. The grey-haired man was also asleep, at the table, and the middle cells as far as I could see were empty with the doors closed. I thought I remembered Homer unlocking the empty cells earlier in the day and I wondered if that was a safety precaution, to add time in case somebody got hold of the keys and tried to lock the jailer in. Or maybe I'd misremembered and he hadn't really used the keys. I had that feeling you sometimes get after a bad dream, that you don't want to go to sleep again right away.

I lay there and waited and tried not to think about anything particular. Things from the past started to go through my head, like before at the beginning of the afternoon, making me go back to when we were all kids, as though I had to say goodbye to it.

I saw Homer come through the entranceway. He didn't make enough noise to wake the other man or the other prisoners, but Jake was suddenly up on his feet. I stayed where I was and half-closed my eyes.

"It's like I am afraid," he said. "They try you together."

"When?" Jake said.

"Now."

"In our absence?"

"Yes. It is going on now, is what I hear. Rumors everywhere, but that is mainly what I hear, and I think is reliable. Also I hear out of all arrest made yesterday only one or two come on any list at all. There was no time. Nobody is going to bother, it's either let them go or try them quick and the charge the same for all, sedition, incitement to violence, treason. You know."

"Both of us together?"

Homer flashed his hand out and said, "All of you, all in here right now. Seven, eight, nine, ten, they do it by the block."

"But we must all be in for different things."

"That's all I know, what I hear."

"Listen," Jake said. "You know we didn't exactly give our right names. I think they've got us mixed up with somebody else."

"Oh, I suspect that, is not that, is not because of any names."

"But the charge is straight theft, isn't it?"

"They don't say. I will tell you soon as I hear more."

He left and Jake sat down. He stayed like that, waiting, and I kept the way I was.

I slept again. Some dreams I have places I go to with fields and mountains, sometimes the sea. And in some dreams I have cities that I've never been to before. But the dream I had this time was just countryside, nothing particular, and I was walking in it and don't remember anything happening.

Jake was sitting the way he'd been before.

"Any idea what time it is?" I said.

"Sun-up, I imagine. It's hard to tell in here."

The other jailer was gone, and the other prisoners still asleep. I felt ghostly and cramped. Jake stretched and did kneebends and told me to do the same, but I couldn't face it. We waited. It began to get lighter and some of the men in the big cell by the entrance stood up and stretched. sat up or lay down again. The light grew, and time dragged.

Then there was some noise outside and people moving around, it sounded like a lot of them, talking and walking through the passageways outside. Once I caught sight of some lumber being carried by some of the military and jail-house guards, down the corridor and past the entranceway.

"Barricades for another riot, I suppose," I said.

Jake held onto the bars and looked at me. Sometimes I've seen him go like that, looking steady as if he's looking straight through the world and out the other side, and it seems to be a face I've never met before but would never forget.

"What?" I said.

"Start doing those bends, Seth. And remember to make the break when I give you the sign."

"I don't see the use—"

"Just do what I say."

Homer came back while I was holding onto the bars and swinging my feet around. Seeing him from the side and then the back when he turned, he looked old and tired, like a different person, not like a man who would enjoy clowning around and laughing. He went over to Jake's cell.

"They decide," he said. Jake nodded.

I stood still to listen and it was so silent I could hear my eyelids creak when I blinked.

"Death," said Homer.

Over his shoulder I saw Jake's face, looking as though he'd known.

"The whole bunch of us?"

"Yes. It is martial law, for all of you."

"How's it going to be?" Jake asked. And Homer told us.

"I send for your families already," he said, and went out again. He hadn't looked at me.

. I shut my eyes and swallowed, and heard it loud in my throat and in my ears.

"What martial law?" I said. "They couldn't have proclaimed it or anything till the riots started, that was hours after they caught us. I can't believe—"

"Hush. It's like he says. You remember what I told you, we'll make the break when they get us in the streets."

Out in the passage somebody started hammering. Soldiers came in and stood around the doorway. Homer came back in once more and talked to the others, the seven men on the right, and the religious nut. The men got up on their feet but the nut didn't seem to have taken anything in. He stood leaning against the bars, looking mopey. The other men began to talk, low and scared. One of them shouted out something just once and afterwards they went back to the same uneasy mutterings.

Guards came in and some of the soldiers were called away. The hammering went on and a sound of chopping, and then a group of people, women, came in and rushed for the right-hand cell. All hell broke loose then: screaming and crying. But I still couldn't believe it.

Two more guards came in, and Maddie and Annie with them. Maddie was running.

She reached me, saying, "They can't do it, Seth, they can't do it," and beat her head against the bars. That was when I believed it; when I held her face up, I saw it there in her eyes and believed it for the first time.

The place was loud as a storm now, it was hard to hear anyone. I said, "Listen, Maddie, we're going to try for a break in the street. But I don't want you there, you hear? You stay away. I specially don't want you there if it won't work. Promise me. It's important. Promise me you'll stay away." I've seen it, mouth open, body twisted out of shape, swollen, suffocated.

"If it happens," I said, "come for the body after."

"Oh no, oh no, no, no," she said, "they can't do it to you, you didn't do anything."

"Promise, Maddie. Nothing's certain, it can go either way whether we get away or not. You stay away, please, I ask it."

"I promise," she said, and cried. A guard came to take her away but she wouldn't go. He lifted her away like a child and she looked back at me all the way. They were taking the other women out, too. One of the guards came for Annie, she was the last, and she hadn't made a sound yet, but when they touched her on the shoulder she crumpled to the floor, sobbing, and put her hands through the bars, holding onto Jake's legs. They carried her out. She was crying like the man who'd killed his wife, and didn't see me when her face was turned in my direction and looking at me.

"How's it going?" Jake said.

"I don't know. My throat's all tight. I got the jitters. I don't know if I'll be much use when it comes time."

"That's all right. Wait for me. Take it easy all the way till I give the sign. Then give it everything you've got for as

83

long as you can. If it don't work out make sure they have to beat the life out of you to stop you getting away. It's better than letting them get us there."

Homer came back and asked Jake if there was anything he wanted done for Annie.

"I say it just in case, because I am married and father and so on. You try to break, yes? There's ten of you, is a chance."

"Don't miss much, do you?"

"Just in case, I keep an eye on her if you want."

"Don't he have any kin?" Jake said, looking over at the religious nut. "Nobody say goodbye to him?"

"I ask him but he keep saying he is the son of God and nobody else."

"Lord, not even a friend. What happened to the man that killed his wife?"

"They take him out in the night."

"Is he being tried quick, like he wanted?" I said.

"No, he is transferred."

"He was arrested after us, wasn't he?"

Homer said yes. "They don't need a trial for that one, he has another knife on him."

"You let him keep a knife on him?" Jake said.

"I see he does not get too close, to me or to the others. He wants the knife, he can keep it."

Jake looked over his head and saw the last of the guards go out the door. The hammering outside had stopped and it was quiet.

"Homer," he said, suddenly, softly, "unlock it. Now."

He looked into Jake's face for a long while. I felt the sweat coming down in floods and thought it must be possible to hear my breathing clear across the floor to the street outside. Homer walked to the table and got his keys and started back to Jake's cell.

He had the key out in his hand when four soldiers and two

of the guards walked in through the entranceway. The guards sat down at the table and one of the soldiers called Homer by name.

"Coming," he said. More came in and stood up against the bars of the empty cells.

"Is too late," he said, and whispered to Jake. Then he said, "I get you fresh water," and went to say something to the soldier, going out afterwards.

"What's happening?" I asked.

Jake said, "Shut up."

We waited. The numbers kept changing in the room. It began to get hot. Finally more were leaving than were coming in, and when Homer came back there were only three left, leaning up against the entranceway, and all the rest were out in the passage, talking.

He came over to us and handed Jake some water through the bars. Then he did the same for me, and I saw he was handing me something else, too: a knife. Then he reached inside his clothes and pulled out a fistful of what looked like leaves.

"No chains, no tying up, I don't think," he said. "But maybe you can't get your hands free. Take these, is for the pain, in case."

"What is that?" Jake said.

"I know a friend get it for me," Homer said, and left, to stop one of the guards who was about to walk over to us and say a word to him. Homer edged him back to the entrance and they talked there.

"What is that?"

"Looks like just leaves." I began to chew them up. All the time I'd thought: don't ever take that stuff, that's the poor man's grave, pretty soon you just live on dope and aren't even hungry any more. Besides, they say it does things to your head, even when you stop and get over the craving for

85

it, you're never right in the head again. I always though it wasn't worth the chance you took.

"What are you doing? Holy God, Seth, it's them African weeds. Don't take it. How much did he give you? It'll knock you right out."

"For the pain," I said, and kept chewing, and wiped the juice off my mouth.

"Are you crazy? Are you out of your mind? Don't take it, it'll kill you, all that amount." He turned around in his cell and slapped his hand against the wall.

When I'd chewed up all the leaves I expected something to happen right away.

"It's all right," I said, "I just feel sort of full and sleepy."

"You fool, you fool, you damn fool," he said. "I'll try my best. Homer says he'll help as much as he can. Hide the knife. If you get your hands free, use it. And if it looks like they've got us for keeps, use it on yourself. Remember."

"Sure," I said, "I'll remember. I feel fine, everything in working order."

He sort of laughed at me and put his hand up to his eyes. "Oh Seth, goddamn," he said, and turned away.

"What's the matter? I'm just fine."

He turned back again and I saw the shine of where tears had been in his eyesockets. I'd never seen him cry before in my life.

"What's wrong, Jake? I know what you're thinking. You're thinking you're going to have to leave me behind."

He didn't answer.

"Want to say goodbye now?"

"Not yet. Do you think you can fight?"

"I don't rightly know. I suppose, when time comes. But I feel fine. I'm not scared any more."

Homer came in and three of the military with him, with an officer in charge. "Those first," the officer said, and

Homer unlocked the big cell on the right, opened the door, and stood back beside it. The two soldiers moved the men out of the cell and more guards came in to hustle them along. One of the men didn't want to leave and sat down on the floor, holding onto the bars. After they'd taken them all out Homer shut the door.

"Not yet," the officer said.

Two more soldiers and two guards came in. Homer told one of the guards to be ready to take over, that he was going as an escort. Then we waited. The guard Homer had spoken to went out and another one came in to take his place.

"I don't think those leaves are all they're made out to be," I said. "Hey, Jake, I said I don't think—"

"I heard you. Take it easy."

We waited some more and then Homer unlocked the cell where the religious nut was. The two guards led him out and he walked quietly enough to the entrance and out. Then he came running in again, with both men holding onto him and his feet sticking out in all directions, it looked like, as they pulled him back and out. He was shouting, "Pharisees, blasphemers!"

There was a lot of noise coming from the passageway, it sounded like there must be about thirty or forty people standing out there, and they laughed as the religious nut was taken through. Then it was our turn. Two soldiers and the officer walked in front and on the sides and Homer and another guard took up the rear. I'd forgotten what the passage looked like, I hadn't noticed much when they'd brought me in. It was lined with soldiers from end to end. As we passed through, Homer handed his keys to the guard he'd spoken to.

We came to the door and stepped out, and I stood stock still, blinded by the sun. I thought we must have been wrong about the time; it felt more like midday than morning. But I couldn't be sure, couldn't be sure about what time it was or what day. It felt like a day that wasn't spaced like others, a day that was running like a river and would always be the same wherever you were set down in it, and might go on for-ever. The other guard jabbed me in the back. "All right," I said, and moved forward, but I was feeling strange, very good but strange, like I was another height of myself above where my feet were going.

We walked down the street and there didn't seem to be too many people around. Some stopped when they saw us and others just looked and kept on walking. Then we came to a knot of people who were shouting things; there were soldiers standing around, and in the middle was the religious nut, bending down, and I thought: they're beating him up and he doesn't know what's happening, I feel sorry for him. But then I caught a look at his face as we passed by. He had on that secret, smug, mealy-mouth look and I realised he was enjoying whatever it was, being in the middle of a fuss.

I noticed that all the sound had blocked out of my ears. It was very strange. My feet kept walking and I could feel Jake very tense beside me. I said, "Jake, you know, the sound's just gone," and I couldn't hear myself say it but I thought it must be coming out slowly and not all formed. He touched my arm, and that was strange, too. It felt like I didn't have skin any more but something else that felt all different. I said, carefully, "I think those leaves are beginning to do something."

Up ahead the seven men and their guard branched off down a street and started to head in the opposite direction from us. We went around a corner. There were more people now, filling up the side of the street and blocking the corners, looking as though they'd been expecting us. I looked behind and saw the guards and soldiers with the religious nut, following along behind. Then I saw somebody throw some-thing but still I couldn't hear. More people began to file into the street till it was like walking between walls of them and I could see their mouths opening and their faces having expressions and their hands moving, shaking fists and cupping around their mouths. Then something else started, like I was going away and coming back again, seeing everything far and small and taking place from below.

And then it happened, suddenly. Like a wall breaking through, it happened far and then it happened near, as if it was all going on inside of me, and the sound came back, loud, people screaming and shouting and calling names and everything near, near. Whatever that stuff was, it hit me all at once, like nothing in this world, making me ten times bigger, lifting me right off the ground so I knew I could do anything, anything at all, I could jump over houses, I could fly. And I shouted.

"Now, Seth, now!" Jake yelled. Homer fell down, taking a soldier and the other guard with him, and I began to fight like it says in the stories when they slew ten thousand, hitting everything. People were yelling, "Get him," and a woman spit in my face and I saw Jake lifted like a swimmer coming up for air and lashing around him, and Annie hitting the officer with a stick and a piece of his tooth fly out, separate, into the air. I was down and being kicked and had dirt in my mouth. Jake called out, "Run, Seth, run, run," and I was up again, running into the crowd. And all at once Maddie was there. I called to her, "Maddie, Maddie," and had my arms out and she pulled me into the crowd, her breast coming into the crook of my arm, lovely and frightening to feel, like when we danced at the wedding. "Seth!" she shouted and they dragged at me from behind and tore me away. I saw the knife fall and took it up quick and hit everything, everybody, it was happening so near and so strong inside, burning and huge, and lifted me away with it, slashing, seeing the red come out. I fell again and I saw Annie, and two of them hitting her, and Jake on the ground with the others pulling him back and beating him on the face, and saw blood from his mouth and nose, and the religious nut screamed and screamed somewhere but I couldn't see him. All of them came down on me all of a heap and dragged me along, about five of them hanging on. Jake was saying, "The hell I will, the hell, lift it yourself you bastard, you son of a bitch." And then I thought how funny it was, how they were going to kill us and Jake had said don't take it, it'll kill you. I started to laugh. They punched me around the head and I still couldn't stop. My knees went under and I sat down in the dust and laughed and laughed. They got me on my feet and I went down again, and then up, laughing, and they had to carry me with my arms all limp, and laughing. Because it was coming from the center and blooming out, enormous all the way through the world, making my arms and legs all laughing too, like my face.

After that I didn't mind, about anything. I thought I had blood on my face but I didn't feel the hurt, and we went forward, the crowd shifting place and changing size, and I'd stopped laughing but I was happy, happier than I knew it was possible, and liking the noise and thinking what a fool I was never to take that stuff before, because I didn't know there were such things in the world and how it makes you feel, so fiercely happy. The procession went on, seeming happy and joyous, as if we were going to some wonderful thing, and all of it more beautiful and exciting than anything else that had ever happened or anything to come after it in the whole history of time. The people and the noise bright and singing and lovely, and strangely wonderful. I could see the sound, real, and I could hear the shape of the people and what the colors did, the inside of me out and free and the outside beautiful and changed, like being a god, and felt good and thought I never knew what it meant before.

Then I was standing and I saw Jake's face altered and large, far away and then near, and the sun and the sky, and a soldier near me.

"There," he said. A lot of people came up close and the military pulled me down to the ground and then everything stood still and at peace. I looked up and saw a soldier's face, I saw the sun on his cheekbone and his eye, spoked with light, perfect and close. I saw him take his arm against the sky and then there was a scream, and I knew it must have come from me though I didn't feel the hurt. But I looked at my hand and there was blood. I heard praying, and I thought it wouldn't be so bad after all.

The holes were there and the stones and they got the ropes on. I started to go up.

"Clear the area," the officer called. "Clear the area."

I went up and I went up and then I fell, all at once I fell. And it began.

You always think it can't go on, it's got to have an end. And I thought maybe I shouldn't have taken those leaves because they say that's what's wrong with it: it lifts you up but it drops you down afterwards lower than you were before. I wondered if that could be why and that was why it was hurting so much. I thought: could it go on like this to the end, never getting less but always more and more? Jake was there and the religious nut, and Jake called, "Goodbye, Seth," and I shouted, "Goodbye, Jake." Then he called to the religious nut, saying, "Goodbye, put in a good word for us when you get there," but he didn't answer.

They say it usually takes three hours. To me it seemed to be more like three days. I passed out and I came back again and I imagined I saw the light go and the stars come out white, very bright and pure. And I could hear my breathing, loud, reaching, as if I was trying to swallow all the cool darkness and its many stars which make you feel so strange and yearning to see, all of them so small and so many and not touching but looking as if there's a life there and a special thought in the way they are spread, specially right and like it could be no other way. It seemed to me I saw the dawn and that I was stiff as though I'd been sleeping in the dew, and that I was wet from making water in the night but hadn't known when it happened and couldn't believe I'd slept, because of the pain.

That was growing more. You hear, they always say, nobody can hurt you that much because when the pain is too sharp your body protects you and makes you numb against it so that the bad part only lasts a short while and after that you know you are over it and it can never be so bad again.

But this was more. I lost the feeling in my arms. Not numb. They had a different feeling now. A no-feeling. And the no-feeling hurt like they say of people who lose an arm or a leg: they will complain of terrible pain in the limb that is no longer there. I thought now, yes, it's happening, and this no-person is coming over me, starting at the edges, and I can feel him coming more and more, closer to the center of me where I still know who I am.

I remember the sun and what it did. Sometimes there were tears on my face, I think, and sweat all the time, and I was half blinded, trying not to look but wanting to now and then to make sure I could still see. Drying up, my eyes were drying up and no place to turn my head. Once there was a vulture moving slow in the air above me and I thought: not my eyes, not my eyes. And I shut them though it would have been no use. There is always something to lose, something that can be taken from you. Even at the end you don't think this is going on forever; nothing else does, so this has to stop too, you think, and at the end I'll be well again. Even when you know.

Three days and two nights I thought it lasted. Pulling and pulling. And a wind roaring in my ears. Not the sound of the crowd—that's my blood going by, like you can hear it jumping in your ear when you lay down your head to sleep.

I tried to moan then, but my voice was taken in my breathing, stretching for the sky with my mouth open and all dry down to my throat and beyond, drying up and burning out like grass on the hillsides in high summer when the sun stands hard above and kills the green out of them. First they go brown and then like ashes, grey. And lastly they are bone-white, skeletons that were once gardens, and the dust blows from them.

I tried to look, to see Jake, but it was like looking into a wall of brass. My eyes opening, heavy and swelled, the glare striking deep into them, and closing up again slowly and not able to shut tight. I thought: it's too late now, I can't call, and it's too hard to look, eyes turning to leather and the no-person weighing down on me, blood falling through my ears.

I thought I heard the other one, the religious maniac, screeching high and thin into the air. And then I heard him clearly. He was starting to pray again, quoting that psalm, saying, "My God, my God, why hast thou forsaken me, why art thou so far from helping me and from the words of my roaring?" And I heard Jake, from where he was, cough. And then I tried, my eyes wincing back from the light, to look, and I saw Jake heave himself and yell, all strangely misshaped like he was singing, "God almighty, why can't you pull yourself together and take it like a man?" And I blacked out again, not knowing whether he'd meant it for himself or for the other one.

When I came to, I thought it must be either dawn or sunset, the air still and calm, and I could open my eyes on it and see.

93

There was a terrible sound coming from somewhere. And then I placed it: the sound I was making in trying to breathe.

The things I knew now, it would almost have been worth it to find them out: how important it is to breathe. You gulp in the air, you fight for it and try to hold onto it and there is no holding.

Strong in the chest, that made me need food. But I knew now, all the things you need in life have to be stolen from somewhere, from the earth or from other people—food, water, warmth, you need them to live. But they can be taken from you. And you can live for a while and can come back to health after you have had fire and food and water taken from you. But the air—take away all the air just for a few moments and life is over. It is death to take that away, because it is free and freely there, the only thing in the world that is truly free. And you live on it as much as you live on food, but do not realise.

I thought I would look down for the last time. But something had happened to my neck and my head; I thought somebody must be holding me and pressing something against me there. I tried to move, and my face was like stone, and all the parts that could make it turn, like iron. I tried and I forced. And I tried it until it worked, stone coming into motion, iron bending, my head sideways, and I could look down.

I saw the hills and the trees and the city beyond, and below me some of the crowd still huddled behind the guards and some looking up, I thought. A shine came off something, a weapon or a helmet, and as I looked to see what it was, a breeze lifted the corner of a soldier's cloak and threw it back over his shoulder, showing the scarlet suddenly like a bird turning wing. I thought: quickly, turn your head back, quickly, or it will stay like this and you won't be able to look up again.

This time it was harder and took much longer. When I had my head up again my eyes were on the religious nut. He was dead by the look of him, and he looked at peace and beyond the moving of any pain. He looked somehow better that way, stretched out, better than he'd looked when he was alive. Being all skin and bones, he seemed to look right there, as though he'd meant to be there all the time and his body had fulfilled itself in the shape it took when he died.

Then I looked at Jake, and a smarting came into my eyes, needing tears. He was dead, you could tell, but not like the other one. You saw the agony of it on him, all of him, the strong body and the open-mouthed face, swollen, wrenched, disfigured with pain. And looking desecrated, shameful to look at, like butchers' meat if they did that to men. I wanted to cry aloud to him, and saw him like it was my own soul I was looking at but more than my soul. And wanted to call to him though he could not hear, hanging as he was bloody-armed from the cross and dead as the other one against the other cross that stood between us on the hill.

I was the last. And this is the last thing, I thought, the last I'll ever see.

I was looking at the sky. I saw it and I knew it as no man ever saw it before, looking into the heart of it, as no other man will ever know it.

I'd never noticed before just how it is, how it is a face that looks back and looks with love, and is arms that open for you. How sweet and calm it is. How blue. How it is lovely beyond belief and goes flying away into farther than can be known. And it goes on like that, on and on. Forever and ever. Without end.